The SECRET of WHITE STONE GATE

ALSO BY JULIA NOBEL

The Black Hollow Lane series
The Mystery of Black Hollow Lane
The Secret of White Stone Gate

Praise for
The Mystery of Black Hollow Lane

"A fast-paced mystery with lots of humor, adventure, and surprising twists! This book has it all: mysterious artifacts, hidden doors, snotty roommates, family secrets, and a wonderful old boarding school with secrets of its own. I absolutely loved it!"

—Jessica Day George, *New York Times* bestselling author of *Tuesdays at the Castle* and *Dragon Slippers*

"A page-turning mystery ripe with plot twists, crackling humor, and a plucky heroine. Kids will love Emmy and beg for more."

—Michael Buckley, *New York Times* bestselling author of the Sisters Grimm series and the N.E.R.D.S. series

"A promising first novel."

—*Booklist*

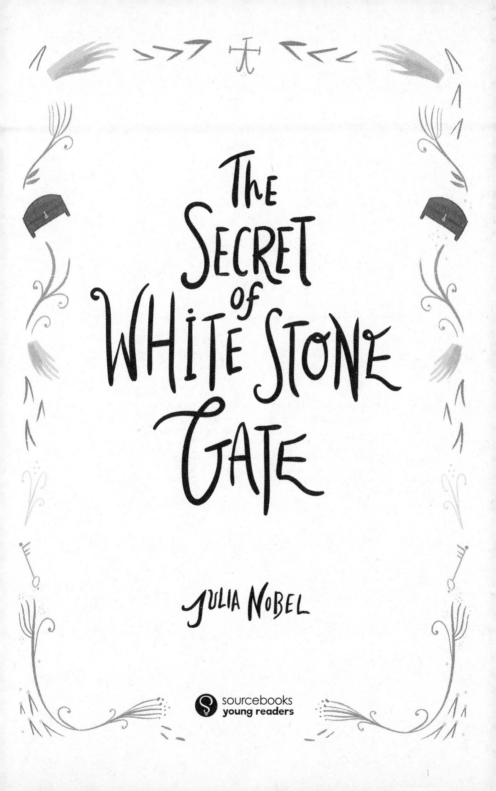

The Secret of White Stone Gate

Julia Nobel

sourcebooks
young readers

For my little girl,
and for my love.
Always.

Chapter 1

The Animal Lover

Lucy was late. Emmy didn't know if that was normal or not, but every time something had gone wrong for Emmy lately, there had been a reason. A bad one. That's why she kept nervously tucking strands of her red hair behind her ear.

The car exhaust and cigarette smoke outside Heathrow Airport in London made her want to wrap her shirt around her nose, and the late-August heat wasn't helping. She checked the time on her phone. Maybe her mom's cousin wasn't a punctual person. *Or maybe…*

Emmy tried to shake some of the tension out of her shoulders. She was being ridiculous. The Order of Black Hollow Lane wasn't after her anymore; she didn't have what they wanted. At least, they didn't *think* she had what they wanted.

Maybe she should give Lucy a call. She was just about to pull up her contact info when the phone started to ring.

"Hello?"

"Darling!"

Emmy smiled. "Hi, Mom."

"How was your flight, dear? Are you completely exhausted?"

"Kinda."

"I bet," her mom said. "Listen, I just got a text from Lucy. She's running a few minutes behind, but she'll be there soon."

Emmy let out a big breath. "Okay, thanks."

"You're really going to love her, Em. She and I had so much fun when we lived together in London."

"Right." Emmy cleared her throat. "I still don't really get why I'm supposed to go to her house during school holidays this year. I mean, it's not like I know her at all."

"She's family, Emmy. You'll get to know her. She and her

husband are involved in all kinds of social clubs and charities, and now that you're going to school in England long-term, I think it would be good for you to make some stronger connections with those types of people."

Those types of people. She meant people with money. And power. After what happened last year, Emmy wasn't too interested in cozying up to powerful people.

"Besides," her mom went on, "I think it'll be good to have family looking after you. It'll be a real load off my mind if I know you're taken care of."

"But I didn't have anyone taking care of me last year, and I was totally fine."

"Really, Emmy?" Her mom's voice was suddenly sharp. "It didn't seem like you were totally fine when you accepted that dare and almost fell out of a bell tower."

"I didn't fall out of a bell tower, Mom. I slipped while I was climbing a rope."

"Well, whatever happened in that tower, you definitely weren't fine."

Emmy cringed. It was true that she hadn't been fine then, but it wasn't because of a dare. Her mom still didn't know what really happened. If she did, she never would have let Emmy come back to Wellsworth.

"Listen," her mom said. "This is part of the deal. If you want to go back to that school, you're going to have Lucy looking after you. Period."

Emmy sighed. "Okay."

"Listen, Em, I know you want to be independent, but you're only twelve."

"Almost thirteen," Emmy corrected her.

"That's still twelve, which is pretty young to be on your own."

Emmy pressed her lips together. Being eleven hadn't stopped Mom from sending Emmy to Wellsworth when she wanted to film a TV show the year before.

"I know you aren't too keen on meeting new people, but Lucy's different. She's family. We used to be really close. She's a great animal lover, did I tell you that? She does some kind of work with dogs."

"Yeah, you told me."

Her mom didn't say anything for a moment. "Well, let me know how things go, okay? You can always come home."

"No!" Emmy said. "I definitely want to be at Wellsworth." And if she had to deal with her mom's cousin to make that happen, she'd just have to suck it up.

"Okay. I love you, Emmy."

"I love you too, Mom."

A few minutes later, a lemon-yellow sports car careened into the parking lot and skidded to a stop. A blond woman got out, yanked off her expensive-looking sunglasses, and examined Emmy.

"Do you belong to Pamela?"

"Uh…I guess so."

"Well, get in, then." Lucy popped the car's trunk and sat back down in the driver's seat without another word.

Emmy tucked her hair behind her ear again. This was the woman her mom had so much fun with in London? She sure seemed different from how her mom had described her.

Emmy heaved her suitcase onto the edge of the trunk and shoved it inside.

"Don't be a brute!" Lucy bellowed. "You'll scratch the paint!"

Emmy snapped the trunk shut. If Lucy was so worried about her car's paint job, she could have helped.

Lucy pulled the car into traffic, and by the time they'd reached the highway, Emmy was trying not to throw up. Lucy drove like a maniac. She flew from one lane to another, making rude hand gestures with perfectly sculpted fingernails and honking the horn like a wild goose. The only part of her face that moved was her bottom lip. Everything else seemed to have been pulled, tucked, and frozen into a permanent scowl.

"So, do you actually talk or what?" Lucy said.

"Oh, um, yeah." Emmy rubbed her hands on her jeans. Talking to strangers wasn't exactly her favorite thing. What kinds of things did adults usually say when they first met? "So, um, what do you do?"

"I breed Chinese cresteds."

Emmy had no clue what that meant. "Chinese what?"

Lucy rolled her eyes. "Dogs," she said, like that was the most obvious thing in the world. "I hear you got into a spot of trouble at school last year."

Emmy's cheeks got hot. "Um, yeah." A spot of trouble. That would be an understatement. Even though she'd spent the last few months in Connecticut, Emmy still got an awful feeling in the pit of her stomach when she thought about what had happened. When she'd gotten to Wellsworth, she'd found out that her dad had gone there, too. A secret school society called the Order of Black Hollow Lane had been after him, which was why he had disappeared when she was three. Emmy and her two best friends had snuck into the Order's secret tunnels to look for proof that the Order had tried to hurt him. Unfortunately, Emmy had gotten caught.

But that wasn't the spot of trouble Lucy was talking about, because no one knew what had really happened except Emmy, her two best friends, and the two teachers who had helped save her. As far as anyone else knew, it was all just a dare that had gone wrong.

"Well, I certainly hope there won't be anything like that this year. I don't want to be the one dealing with all that rubbish. I hear they've hired a new head of security, so hopefully she'll do a better job at keeping you kids under control."

"She?" Emmy would breathe easier if the new security person was a woman. The Order was a strict "boys only" club.

"Yes, I read all about it in that school newsletter your mother signed me up for. I guess the last fellow quit at the end of the year."

Emmy shivered. She always did that when she thought about the old head of security, Jonas. She had trusted him, but he was the one who had caught her in the tunnels, chased her into the belfry of an old church, and tried to kill her. All because of something that was sitting in her backpack right now. She clutched her bag tighter. She would probably regret bringing the box of medallions with her, but she liked having it close. As far as Jonas and the Order were concerned, it was destroyed. If they found out differently... Well, there was no turning back now.

After what seemed like the longest car ride ever, they finally made it to Lucy's house in one piece.

"Don't touch anything," Lucy said as she opened the front door. "Georgian town houses cost a fortune in London, especially when they're in such perfect condition."

Emmy looked around. No art. No family photos. No comfy chairs. Apparently "perfect condition" meant "stuffy old box."

"Your room's up on the next floor," Lucy said. "It's the little one at the end." She banged on a door next to the entryway. "Harold? Are you in there?"

A grunt sounded from behind the door. *That must be Lucy's husband.*

"Did the paperwork come from the club yet?" she asked.

Another grunt. This one must have meant no because Lucy crossed her arms and sighed.

"We've been offered membership in the Thackery Club," she said smugly. "It's the most prestigious club in the country, you know."

Emmy wasn't sure what could be so prestigious about a club, but from the way Lucy was smirking, it must have been a big deal.

"A couple members popped over for tea the other day

and offered us exclusive pricing at their electronics store. Harold and I already got brand new cell phones for next to nothing."

"There are *people* in the lounge," Harold said, as though these "people" were some kind of pests that had weaseled through the door.

"What people?" Lucy bellowed.

"For the girl."

It was like someone had dumped ice water down Emmy's back. Someone was here for her. More than one someone. Were they from the Order? She'd always known it would be risky to come back to the UK, back to the school where Jonas had tried to kill her, but she figured she'd be safe now that they believed she didn't have the box.

"They're in the lounge," Harold said.

Lucy opened the door on Emmy's left. It was too late to run now.

Before Emmy could back away, a short, stocky girl with a black ponytail barreled through the door and practically tackled Emmy in a huge bear hug. "What took you so long? We've been waiting on that lumpy sofa for ages."

All of Emmy's fear melted away. "Hey, Lola." It felt good to hug her best friend again.

Lola pulled away and gave Emmy a serious look. "You've been doing drills this summer, right?"

Emmy rolled her eyes and nodded.

"'Cause trials are in two weeks, and Madam Boxgrove is going to get after you if your left foot isn't a bit faster when you're dribbling."

"I promise, I've been practicing!" Emmy shook her head. Leave it to Lola to ask her about soccer when they hadn't seen each other in two months.

Emmy looked over Lola's shoulder and saw a tall woman with wild, black hair. She leaned on her cane and smiled. "Lola's been talking about you all summer. At least, that's what her dad tells me."

Emmy ran over and gave Lola's mom a hug. Madam Boyd was in charge of Emmy and Lola's house at Wellsworth, but over the course of the year, she'd come to mean a lot more to Emmy than just a housemistress.

"As touching as this little reunion is," Lucy said, "I'm going upstairs to tend to Mr. Minicomb."

"Who's Mr. Minicomb?" Lola asked Emmy.

Emmy shrugged.

"You don't mind if I take the girls out for a bit, do you?" Madam Boyd asked Lucy.

Lucy just waved her hand and didn't look back, which Emmy assumed meant yes.

"We'll get your things settled in your room first," Madam Boyd said. Emmy and Lola each grabbed one of Emmy's suitcases and heaved them up the staircase.

They passed two large bedrooms that didn't look lived-in before they reached the little door at the end. The room was so tiny they could barely wedge the suitcases between the bed and the wall.

Lola snorted. "Guess you got the maid's room."

Emmy didn't really care. It was only a week until she went back to Wellsworth. Just the thought of being back at school sent a warm rush through her. Wellsworth was where she belonged.

"Right, then," Madam Boyd said, "let's get going."

Emmy tried to cover up a groan. She just wanted to crash. "Can I have a nap first?"

Madam Boyd peered out into the hallway and then snapped the bedroom door shut. "Sorry, this can't wait. Your father has a job for you."

Chapter 2

The Royal Bank of London

Emmy stared at Madam Boyd. "You know about my dad?" The last she'd heard, it was only her humanities teacher, Master Barlowe, who knew her dad was still alive.

"After the…incident at the end of last year, your father thought it best to have more than one person at school who knew the full extent of the situation," Madam Boyd said. "Since I'm your head of house, I can keep an extra eye out for your safety." She looked at Lola and narrowed her eyes. "And make sure you both stay out of trouble."

"Have you seen him?" Emmy asked.

Madam Boyd shook her head. "Thomas and I have ways of communicating, but I never know where he is. It's just not safe."

Emmy's shoulders slumped. That's what Master Barlowe had said, too. If her dad could communicate with Boyd and Barlowe, why couldn't he communicate with her? Sending her a few cryptic letters last year definitely didn't count.

"He'd like you to come with me to the Royal Bank of London," Boyd said. "There's a safe-deposit box there that he'd like you to open. And he said—and I'm assuming you know what this means, because I have no idea—that if you saved any of his relics, please bring them along."

Emmy looked at Lola. They both knew exactly what Thomas meant.

The medallions.

Her father had stolen them years ago. He knew the medallions would open the Order's secret vaults, and he didn't want Jonas to get all the valuable artifacts inside. Emmy found the medallions before she went to Wellsworth, and when Jonas had cornered her, she pretended to throw them into the North

Sea. Only Emmy, Lola, and their friend Jack knew that Emmy still had them. At least, that's what Emmy had thought. Her dad must have guessed that she'd try to save them.

Emmy clutched at the straps on her backpack. "I have everything I need. Let's go."

A short while later, the three of them clambered into a black taxicab, Madam Boyd in the front, the girls in the back.

"Royal Bank of London on St. Martin's le Grand," Boyd told the driver. The cab lurched into traffic, and they started winding their way through the endless lines of cars headed downtown. "I'm afraid you'll have to suffer through a bit of sightseeing after. Just in case someone's...keeping an eye on us. We don't want them to think too much about us stopping at the bank."

"Did you get my last text?" Lola asked, completely ignoring the fact that her mom had just said that someone might be following them.

"About Jack?" Emmy asked.

Lola nodded.

"Yeah. Sounds like he's ready for summer to be over." Jack was their other best friend, and spending time with his family wasn't his favorite thing.

Emmy leaned closer to Lola. "Do you know if his dad has

said anything about…you know?" she asked. Jack's father and older brothers were part of the Order. It made his friendship with Emmy a lot more complicated.

"I don't think he's told me anything he hasn't told you," Lola said. "Both his older brothers are still living at home, which isn't exactly comfy. He's excited that Oliver's starting at Wellsworth, though."

"Oh right, that's his younger brother, isn't it?"

"Yeah. Jack's hoping he can steer him away from you-know-what and generally keep him in line. I told him I'd help since I have such a great record of obedience." She winked.

Emmy grinned and put her head on Lola's shoulder. Two months of text messages were no substitute for actually being together.

Emmy hadn't been in a car in London before, but it was a lot like the few times she'd been to New York City: lots of people, lots of cars, and nobody seemed to be getting very far. Finally, they crawled to a stop outside a rambling stone building.

"Here ya are, ladies," the driver said. Emmy and Lola scrambled out of the cab while Madam Boyd paid the driver. The building was five stories high and made of thousands of gray and white stones. At the top was a fancy balcony that wound its way around the building, which took up an entire city block.

Emmy and Lola followed Madam Boyd inside. Instead of more stone, they were surrounded by dark wood that was so shiny it looked like someone polished it every day. They waited in line for one of the two dozen tellers to call them forward. The longer they waited, the more Emmy's fingers twitched. What was in that safe-deposit box? And what did her dad want her to do with it?

"Next," said a teller at the end.

Emmy, Lola, and Madam Boyd walked up to the desk. Emmy tried to focus on the bank teller's kind face and not the knots in her stomach, but it wasn't working.

"What can I do for you today?" the teller asked.

"We're here to access a safe-deposit box," Madam Boyd said as she handed the woman a key and an identification card. "Under the name Margaret Boyd."

"Okay, it looks like everything is in order here. I just need to get the manager so we can go back to the vaults."

The teller came back with another woman. "You can come back," she said.

They followed her down the hallway, past offices and meeting rooms until they finally reached a heavy-looking door with a keypad beside it. The teller and the manager both entered codes and the door swung open, revealing a long line of new doors. These ones were huge and round, and there were two combination locks in between each one.

"Stay here, please," the manager said. She and the teller walked down to a door and each of them started clicking the combination locks into place. A loud *clack* echoed off the concrete. The manager turned the metal rods on the front of the door and it slowly eased open.

"Only one of you can enter the vault," she said. "I can stay out here with the children if you—"

"No," Madam Boyd said, "this is Emmy's box." She pushed Emmy forward. "She's the only one who should go in."

The teller and the manager looked at each other. Part of Emmy hoped the manager would say no. Then she wouldn't have to deal with whatever was inside.

The manager held a key out, dictating "Number 847."

Emmy took a deep breath and walked in.

The vault was brighter than she expected, and bigger, too. There were rows and rows of thin boxes built into the walls. Number 847 was on the bottom, which was the only row with boxes that were tall enough to fit more than paper or jewelry. Somehow that made Emmy more nervous, like having a bigger box meant bigger trouble. She crouched down, put the key in the lock, and turned.

The box opened easily. It was lined with green velvet, and inside was a single piece of paper. She picked it up with a shaking hand and started to read:

Dear Emmeline,
If you have any relics, please leave them here.
You've carried them long enough.
Sincerely,

A friend

Emmy turned the page over. That was it. That's all her dad wanted. The medallions. It was always about the medallions.

She didn't know what else she was expecting. She should have been relieved that there wasn't some dangerous task, or something else that would throw her in the Order's way again, but if he could find a way to leave a letter in this safe-deposit box, why couldn't he leave something more meaningful?

She was about to take the medallions out of her bag when she saw something else, something that had been hidden under the letter. It was a photograph. And it made Emmy's insides crawl.

Two young men stood with their arms around each other's

shoulders. They looked like they were laughing at some inside joke that only the two of them knew. One man was her father. The other was Jonas.

Anger and confusion boiled under Emmy's skin. Why would her dad leave this picture for her? What kind of message was it supposed to send? She turned the picture over and found her father's scrawling handwriting on the back:

We were best friends. We still betrayed each other. Trust no one.

Emmy's eyes got blurry. She didn't want to not be able to trust anyone. She didn't want to be suspicious of her friends— the only real ones she'd ever had. This whole situation was her dad's fault. So why should she trust *him*?

Her dad wanted the box of medallions, just like Jonas did. How did she know his motives were any better than the Order of Black Hollow Lane?

She looked at the instructions on the paper again. The medallions would be safe from the Order here. Her dorm room wasn't exactly burglar proof. She'd thought about leaving them in Connecticut, but what if the Order broke into her mom's house? She brought them along because there wasn't much of a choice, but life would be a lot easier if she didn't have to worry about the Order searching her room again.

The two people in the picture seemed to be staring at her. *Trust no one*, her dad had said. Obviously, her dad had access to this vault, and she wasn't ready to hand the medallions over to him. Not yet.

Emmy took the picture so her dad would know she'd been here, then slid the box closed and stepped outside.

"May I have a safe-deposit box of my own, please?" she asked.

"Unfortunately, children are not allowed to obtain their own safe-deposit boxes," the manager said. "An adult must open one for you."

"That'll be fine," Madam Boyd said.

"Can it be in a different vault?" Emmy asked.

The bank manager and teller looked at each other. "If you wish," the manager said slowly.

They went back to the front desk and filled out all the paperwork. Emmy paid with the credit card her mom had given her for emergencies. She didn't know what she'd tell her mom, but she'd figure out something. The teller and manager took them back to the vault room, and Emmy unlocked her new safe-deposit box. Her fingers trembled on her backpack zipper. Was she really ready to say goodbye to this box? She'd almost died for it last year. And if she left it here, it would mean no more exploring in the tunnels under the school.

She slipped the box into the velvet and traced her fingers against it one more time. Then she closed the safe-deposit box and locked it up tight. She was done exploring. It was time to put the Order behind her.

Chapter 3

Wellsworth

Emmy tried to put the box out of her mind for the next few days. Lola and Madam Boyd took her all around London, which was the perfect distraction. Lucy didn't seem to care where Emmy went as long as she was out of the house and away from her dog. If you could call Mr. Minicomb a dog. He was completely hairless except for a few wispy strands of fur that sprouted out of his paws like wheat grass. Lucy held him close to her chest every time

Emmy came into the room, like she was infected with some kind of American dog disease. On Sunday morning, Lucy dropped Emmy off at the train station with barely a goodbye. Emmy hitched her backpack higher on her shoulder. Maybe she could convince her mom to let her stay at school for the holidays.

The station was buzzing with people. Emmy recognized a lot of them from school, which was a relief. She'd rarely taken the train, and never by herself. She wished she could have gone to school with Lola a few days earlier, but Emmy's mom had insisted on her spending more "bonding time" with Lucy. Like that was even possible.

"Emmy!"

Natalie Walsh was running over, her blond curls bouncing behind her. Natalie threw her arms around Emmy. "Did you have a good summer?"

"It was okay, I guess." It had been pretty boring, so there wasn't much to tell.

Natalie pointed a finger at Emmy. "You've been practicing, right?"

Emmy grinned. Natalie was in fourth year like Emmy, and they'd both been on the Wellsworth soccer team the year before. "I promise I've been practicing."

"Good. We'll have to replace Manuela and Mariam. I hope we find some good players."

Emmy sat with Natalie on the train, along with Cadel, who had been Jack's roommate the year before. Jack was being driven to school, so it was nice to sit with some other friends. The front two train cars were packed with Wellsworth students, most of whom were catching up and telling stories from their summers.

There was one boy reading a book by himself. He looked like he was in fourth or fifth year, but Emmy didn't recognize him. He pushed some floppy blond hair out of his eyes and smiled at something he was reading. Emmy's stomach fluttered in a way that it usually only did for famous, good-looking soccer players. She cleared her throat and looked away. She didn't know everyone at Wellsworth, but she definitely would have remembered that fluttering if she'd seen this boy before.

When the train pulled into the town of King's Lynn, students dragged their luggage onto the buses that would take them up the coast to Wellsworth. Emmy smiled when she saw the person standing next to the closest bus.

"Hi, Master Barlowe," she said.

"Good afternoon, Miss Willick," he said with a broad smile. Master Barlowe had helped her a lot with her studies the year before, but as it turned out, he'd been watching out for her safety, too. He knew her dad and knew the Order might come after her. "I trust you've had a good summer?"

"Yes, sir."

"Did you get on all right with your humanities homework? I know Madam Boyd and I left you with quite the workload."

That was an understatement. Emmy had to do an entire year's worth of coursework over the summer so she could catch up on all the English history she'd never learned in America.

"I think I did okay," Emmy said.

Master Barlowe smiled. "Excellent. Let's set up a time when I can take a look at your work and discuss any other…uh… issues that might have come up over the break."

Emmy's fingers twitched. Did he know that her dad suspected the medallions hadn't been destroyed? Or did he have another message from her dad, like Madam Boyd? She nodded and got onto the bus, trying to look as relaxed as she could. She couldn't let any Order members suspect that she and Master Barlowe had anything to talk about other than schoolwork.

The bus ride wasn't long, and soon they were pulling into the Wellsworth driveway. The spires of the old Blacehol Abbey towered over the rest of the main building, which sprawled out awkwardly across the landscape. Emmy's whole body felt suddenly warm. She was home.

It took forever to haul her suitcase to Audrey House, but she finally heaved it up to the fourth flour and into her new room. She was surprised to see Natalie putting clothes in the closet, and Lola lying on the bed.

"Guess what!" Natalie said. "We're roommates this year!"

Emmy grinned. Spending the year with Natalie would be a lot better than spending it with Victoria, her stuck-up roommate from the year before.

"Who are you with?" Emmy asked Lola.

"Jaya," she said without looking up from her phone. "That should be good."

Emmy unzipped her suitcase. "I guess you unpacked a few days ago."

"Yup," Lola said. "I mean, I chucked my suitcase in the closet, which is pretty much the same thing."

"How are you going to find anything?" Natalie asked.

"What's there to find?" Lola said. "You grab something gray, you grab something green, get a fresh pair of knickers, and you're ready for the day."

Emmy looked at Natalie and they both rolled their eyes.

"Why don't you go find Jack?" Emmy asked.

"Who do you think I've been talking to all afternoon?" Lola said as she punched something into her phone.

"Who's his roommate this year?" Emmy asked warily. Jack had trouble with his first-year roommate. Brynn, who happened to be Lola's cousin, had made Jack's life miserable when he found out Jack wouldn't be joining the Order like the rest of the boys in his family.

"Some new kid," Lola said. "Sam something or other."

Emmy tucked her hair behind her ear. Maybe Sam was the one she'd seen on the train.

"Jack got permission to take sixth- and seventh-year art classes this year," Lola said.

"Seriously?"

Lola nodded. "He's pretty chuffed."

Emmy smiled. After a year in the United Kingdom, Emmy had figured out that *chuffed* meant *excited*, but it had taken her a while to get used to all the British slang.

"I bet his dad's not so chuffed," Emmy said. Mr. Galt was an art dealer, but he wanted Jack to be involved in the business side of art, not the actual creation of it.

"Who cares?" Lola said. "He'll probably have to do some kind of directed study for art next year, 'cause he's going to run out of classes soon."

Emmy and Natalie spent the rest of the afternoon setting up their room, which Lola constantly told them was taking too long.

Emmy hung her last skirt in the closet. "There, done."

Lola threw her head back and groaned. "Finally! I'm starving. Let's grab Jack and get some food."

"I'm meeting Jaya for supper," Natalie said. "I'll catch up with you later."

Lola sent Jack another text, and she and Emmy met him in the common room.

"Hey!" Emmy gave him a hug. "You got new glasses!"

Jack touched the rims of his glasses, which were still square-shaped but were thinner and bright blue. "Yeah, I could barely see out of the other ones, they were so scratched up. Did you get a haircut?"

"Yeah, I—"

"Okay, okay," Lola said, pushing them toward the door. "Everybody looks brilliant. Now get a move on."

"Just wait." He looked over his shoulder. "Oli, come meet Emmy."

A boy ducked his head and shuffled toward them. "Hi."

"Hi Oliver," Emmy said. With his well-combed hair and round glasses, Oliver looked like a much neater version of Jack.

"You can sit with us at supper if you like," Jack said, "but you might want to meet some of the other first years instead. You know, make some friends."

Oliver nodded, but his eyes were so wide it was like Jack had said "meet the sharks" instead of "make some friends."

The Hall was as loud as ever that night, with the sounds of clanking cutlery and shrill laughter bouncing off the old stone walls. It had been the Blacehol Abbey Cathedral once, but now it was basically just a fancy dining hall. Emmy breathed in all the familiar smells: buttery biscuits, garlicky mashed potatoes, spicy dal with naan bread. She couldn't wait to dive into a flaky Cornish pasty.

When they were all stuffed, Emmy, Jack, and Lola made their way slowly back to their common room. The double-sided fireplace blazed in the middle of the room, cutting through the damp chill that leaked through the old window-sills. Madam Boyd was there; since she was the head of Audrey House, she must have been there to greet the new students. The other teacher in the room was a bit of a surprise, and seeing him again made Emmy squirm.

"What's Larraby doing here?" Emmy asked. Master Larraby was in charge of Latin Society, which was like a recruiting ground for the Order. He had never threatened her, but he definitely made her uncomfortable.

"He's head of Edmund House," Jack said.

"I know, but he never comes in the common room." She lowered her voice. "He doesn't exactly go out of his way to help his students."

Jack gave her a wry smile. "It's a requirement. Everybody has a meeting with their heads of houses on the first night."

"I keep forgetting that you missed the start of last year," Lola said.

Most of the squashy chairs and couches were full, so they found seats at a table. Lola whipped a pack of cards out of her coat pocket. "Come on, we can squeeze in a game of Slap It before the meeting starts."

It had taken Emmy a while to learn the game Lola had invented, but now she could steal cards and slap stacks almost as well as Lola. Natalie and Jaya joined in after the first round, but before they could deal the cards for the second, Madam Boyd stepped to the fireplace and cleared her throat.

"All right," she said, "settle down now."

The room got quiet pretty quickly, except for the corner where Master Larraby was talking with some of the boys from Latin Society. Larraby laughed loudly. He didn't seem to have noticed Madam Boyd talking.

Her jaw went tight. "Master Larraby." It seemed like she

was trying not to grit her teeth. "Won't you join me in welcoming our students back to school?"

He put up one finger as if to say "just a minute." Madam Boyd's lips were getting whiter and whiter. Her temper was almost as quick as Lola's, and she definitely didn't like to be kept waiting.

Finally, the boys all laughed—Larraby must have finished his story, because Master Larraby finally strolled over to the fireplace. "So sorry, Boyd, please, go ahead."

Madam Boyd stared at him a moment longer and then turned to the group. "For those of you who are new to Wellsworth, welcome. I am Madam Boyd and I'm head of Audrey House."

"And I'm Master Jameson Larraby," Larraby said. "I am, of course, head of Edmund House, and I am also a graduate of Cambridge, chair of our school's Latin Department, and head of the Latin Society. I hope to see some of the new Edmund lads join our Latin Society soon. We're always looking for new blood."

Emmy looked at Lola and rolled her eyes. Latin Society may not be able to have an official boys-only policy, but they made sure no girl wanted to stay very long.

"Your schedules will be in your mailboxes tomorrow

morning," Boyd said. "New students will have a consultation scheduled with either myself or Master Larraby sometime this week. Also, the Wellsworth Annual Charity Supper is coming up in a few weeks, and this year Audrey and Edmund House will be hosting. We will need a committee of volunteers, so I'll leave a sign-up sheet on the bulletin board. If all the slots aren't filled by tomorrow evening, I'll start adding your names for you."

"That's democratic," Lola scoffed in a voice that wasn't very quiet.

Madam Boyd glared at her daughter. "Ah, I see we have our first volunteer. Miss Boyd, thank you for being our committee chairperson."

Lola's jaw dropped. "What?"

"Remember," Boyd went on as if Lola hadn't said anything, "at Wellsworth we expect nothing short of excellence, both in academics and in personal choices."

"Wait," Lola said. "I'm not—"

"If you are struggling in either of those areas," Boyd said loudly, "come see one of us immediately so we can get things straightened out. I would wish you good luck, but with hard work and self-discipline you won't need it. Have a good term."

Chairs scraped on the floor as people stood up, and Madam Boyd walked toward a group of first years.

"Hang on, Mum," Lola said. "I'm not chairing some committee."

Madam Boyd put up her hand. "Save it, Lola. I'll get you an access code for the student conference room and the notes from last year's committee." She smiled. "And maybe next time you'll save your sass for someone else."

Lola stomped her foot and groaned. "This is totally unfair." She pointed her finger at Emmy and Jack. "You two had better be the first ones on that sign-up sheet."

"Don't worry, we'll do it," Jack said.

"Can I help?" someone said from behind them.

Emmy's stomach fluttered. It was the boy from the train.

"Sure, that'd be great," Jack said. "This is Sam, he's my roommate. This is Emmy, and that's Lola."

"Hey." He flashed them a grin and Emmy prayed no one would notice her cheeks getting hot.

Jack went over to the sign-up sheet. "Um, sorry Lola, but we won't be the first ones signing up."

"Why? Who else is on there?"

"Brynn." Emmy's chest got tight. Brynn was part of the Order, and he'd spent a lot of time trying to intimidate Emmy the year before. He couldn't stand Jack or Lola either, even though Lola was his cousin.

"Why would a selfish git like Brynn want to help with a charity supper?" Lola asked.

"Maybe he needs volunteer hours," Sam said.

"Not a chance," Jack said. "He's up to something."

Emmy shuddered. If Brynn was up to something, that was never a good sign.

Chapter 4

New Friends and Old Enemies

Emmy's alarm seemed to go off extra early the next morning. She'd pretty much gotten used to the time change when she was at Lucy's, but she'd also gotten used to sleeping in. She pressed snooze on her phone and rolled over.

Somebody jiggled her shoulder.

"Come on, sleepy," Natalie said, "we've got to figure out our schedules before first bell."

Emmy yawned and sat up in bed. She'd been wondering who

her teachers would be all summer. She still wanted Barlowe for humanities, but when it came to Latin, she'd be thrilled with anybody other than Larraby.

She threw on her uniform, brushed her hair and teeth, and hurried downstairs. The common room was filled with people pouring over slips of paper they'd grabbed out of their mailboxes.

"You've got to be kidding," a sixth-year boy said. "I'm stuck with Wilbert again. His lectures put me straight to sleep. How am I supposed to pass chemistry?"

"Algebra in first block?" a seventh-year girl said. "I can't do equations first thing in the morning."

"Who's Ms. Parker?" asked an anxious-looking first year. "Is she hard? I've never taken geography before."

Emmy grabbed the schedule in her mailbox. Economics, earth and ocean science, art, design and technology, applied mathematics, Latin, and humanities. She looked at the teachers and held her breath: Barlowe for humanities, and Ellenby for Latin. She breathed out and smiled. Without Larraby, she'd be even further away from the Order's orbit.

"WHAT?"

Emmy looked up. Lola was staring at her schedule like it had personally insulted her.

"I've got physics and chemistry in the same semester?" Lola said. "That's just cruel!"

"Don't complain," Jack said as he walked over to them. "I've got to finish all of sixth-year history of art in one semester so I can do seventh-year in the spring."

Lola rolled her eyes. "You're the one who asked for advanced art classes, and it's your favorite subject, so stop griping."

"Let's go eat," Emmy said.

"Oh, um, I kind of told Sam I'd wait for him," Jack said. "It's okay if he sits with us, right?"

"Of course," Lola said.

Emmy's ears felt hot. It was definitely okay with her if Sam sat with them.

They waited another minute until Sam finally came down the stairs. Emmy tucked her hair behind her ear. Wellsworth's gray and green sweater Sam wore made his hazel eyes seem even brighter.

"Hey," he said, "it's Lola and Emmy, right?"

Emmy nodded. *Please don't blush, Emmy, please don't blush.* Saying that in her head over and over seemed to make her face even hotter.

He grabbed his schedule, and they all walked down the forest path and into the wide grass fields that led to the main building.

"That's the fine arts building," Jack said as he pointed to a building nearby, "and the science building's down there. The performance art building is way on the other side of the Hall. You can't even see it from here."

They filled up their plates at the food table and sat down. Emmy saw a lot of familiar faces, especially from her soccer team. Just thinking about playing again made her feet tingle and twitch.

Her old roommate Victoria was sitting across the Hall. Emmy had seen her in the common room the night before, but she'd ignored her. Victoria had been horrible last year, and as far as Emmy was concerned, the more they stayed away from each other, the better.

Lola nudged her. "That's the new head of security," she said quietly.

Emmy followed her gaze. A woman in a sharp suit was sitting with some of the teachers. "Do you know anything about her?"

"I've talked to her a couple of times," Lola said. "She seems friendly enough. She was a colonel in the army. Apparently, she trained people in martial arts."

Emmy glanced at Sam, then turned toward Lola so he wouldn't hear. "She can't be part of you-know-what, right? 'Cause they only allow guys to join."

"Well, she's got to at least know something, don't you think? I mean, there are security cameras everywhere. She's bound to notice people disappearing behind secret doors."

Emmy's stomach twisted. She hadn't thought of that. The idea of another Order member being able to watch her every move was pretty unnerving.

Jack and Sam both pushed their chairs back from the table.

"You'd better finish up," Jack said. "First bell's in five minutes."

Emmy looked at her half-eaten plate of food and pushed it away. She wasn't hungry anymore.

Emmy's first few classes seemed like they'd be a lot of work, but she didn't feel the same kind of panic about being behind like she had the year before. Her new Latin teacher walked them through some new concepts in class, which was a welcome change from Larraby. All he did was talk with his favorite students and assign worksheets. How he'd ever ended up as the head of the department was a mystery to her.

She didn't have any classes with Jack or Lola until humanities.

"Budge up, will you?" Lola said as she slid onto a bench next to Emmy. "I told Jack I'd save space for him and Sam."

Emmy squeezed against the end of the bench and pretended to be more interested in her pencil than she was with the fact that Sam would be sitting with them again.

Sam and Jack slipped into the classroom right before Barlowe closed the door.

"Cutting it close, gentlemen," Barlowe said as he trotted down the stairs toward the stage.

"This classroom is wild," Sam whispered as he and Jack sat down.

He was right. Emmy was used to it by now, but on her first day, the rounded benches that looked down on a sunken stage had been like walking into an Ivy League college class.

"Welcome to another year in humanities," Barlowe said. "I see we have a couple of new students, so let me remind everyone that at Wellsworth, we believe that classes like literature, history, and ethics should be studied together, as they are all deeply connected. This year we'll be focusing on the English Civil War and the Restoration period. We'll talk about how philosophical and religious changes in England contributed to the war, and how the war itself led to even more social change. As England slowly became a more tolerant society, its writers and artists became bolder political critics."

Jack's eyes lit up and he raised his hand. "We talk about that a lot in art history. Art can have a huge impact on society, because it can make statements and generate debate in the most amazing ways! Even in dictatorships artists find ways to—"

"Um, Master Barlowe?" Lola interrupted. "You should know that if you let Jack get going about art, he'll take over the whole class."

Jack bit his lip, but he smiled and laughed along with everyone else.

"We do have quite a bit to cover today, but thank you, Mr. Galt. Perhaps I could ask you to give a presentation on Restoration-period artists this term."

Jack's eyes went wide. "Yes, sir."

Jack was still smiling by the time dinner rolled around. Emmy was thrilled that he'd had such a good first day. He'd spent most of his first three years at Wellsworth in the Order's shadow, what with his older brothers being members and Brynn giving him such a hard time. But Malcolm and Vincent had both left school now, and Brynn seemed less and less interested in picking on him. Maybe Jack would finally be able to stand out on his own.

Emmy, Jack, and Lola found three seats together, since Sam had a meeting with Larraby.

"Did you warn Sam that Larraby won't help him one jot?" Lola asked Jack as she cut into her fish pie.

"Yeah," Jack said, "I told him we'd help him get settled. I think he's a bit more nervous than he's letting on. He's never been to a boarding school before."

Emmy could relate to that. Wellsworth had been so intimidating during her first few weeks. Now she couldn't imagine being anywhere else.

Lola leaned in closer. "Do you think Larraby's got more stuff to do with you-know-what now that Jonas has gone?" Jonas had high-tailed it out of Wellsworth after Emmy had escaped from him.

"Maybe," Jack said. "I'm sure Jonas is still in charge. The Order isn't just a Wellsworth thing anymore."

Emmy pressed her lips together. She didn't like thinking about Order members being part of the regular world. There could be members anywhere and she'd never know. At least at Wellsworth they were almost all sixth- and seventh-year boys, apart from Brynn, and they were all part of the Latin Society. It was a lot easier to keep track of who might be involved.

"Even if Jonas is still Brother Loyola, there's got to be

someone who runs things here," Lola said. "Somebody's got to lead meetings and check out recruits."

"I don't care what Larraby's doing as long as he leaves me out of it," Emmy said. "I'm done with the Order."

"Me too," Jack said.

Lola took another bite of pie.

"Um, Lola?" Emmy said.

"Hmm?"

"You're done with them too, right?"

"Well, obviously I can't do much snooping around without you two," she grumbled.

Emmy rolled her eyes and smothered her bun in butter. Leave it to Lola to miss tangling with a dangerous society.

Madam Boyd came up to their table. "I've got all the information about last year's fundraiser in my office," she said to Lola. "Come see me after supper and we'll go over it." She walked away before she could hear Lola complain.

Lola shoved her fork into her pie. "Like I don't have enough to do."

"Think of all the extra time you'll have now that we're not researching the Order," Jack said.

"I'd rather sneak around than work on a committee with Brynn."

Emmy looked at her plate. It was all well and good for Lola to wish she could dig into the Order's secrets. They'd never gone after her.

When Emmy got back to her room that night, she pulled out the letters her father had sent her the year before. The first one had led her to the box of medallions that he'd hidden in the attic of their Connecticut farmhouse. The second one was older, it talked about a meeting between her dad and Brother Loyola. If he hadn't sent her that one, she never would have made the connection between her dad and the Order. As for the third letter, she still shuddered when she read Master Barlowe telling her father that the Order was searching for him and he needed to go on the run.

Emmy didn't read the fourth letter. She knew it by heart.

Forgive my cryptic notes, they could have fallen into the wrong hands.

Forgive me pretending to be a priest, I was desperate to catch a glimpse of you.

I won't ask you to forgive my absence, even though it haunts me.

She put the letters in their box under her bed and wrapped

herself in her blanket. Could she forgive her dad being absent from her life for so long? He had left to protect her and her mom, to keep the Order away from them. So why did he send her all those clues that led her straight to the Order last year?

Emmy flicked off her lamp and shut her eyes as tight as she could. There was no point in thinking about it anymore. She wasn't going to let the Order—or her father—mess up another year at Wellsworth.

Chapter 5

The Charity Supper

Emmy got her charity binder out of her bag and sat in the corner of the common room. She and Sam had been trying to get donations for the silent auction for two weeks, and it was a relief to be almost done. Sam came down the Edmund stairs and sat across from her. They'd been working together so much that Emmy had gotten used to the stomach fluttering. Every once in a while, if Sam made her laugh or accidentally brushed her hand, she'd feel a giant swoop behind her belly-button. Those swoops seemed to have a direct connection to her ears, making them hot and flushed. Thank goodness she could hide her ears behind her hair.

"Did your mom send those tickets?" Emmy asked as she opened her binder.

Sam counted on his fingers. "She got the London Symphony Orchestra, James Ehnes, and the Doric String Quartet."

"Nice," Emmy said, even though she didn't have a clue who any of those people were.

"Yep," Sam said with a grin. "I guess having a classical music promoter for a mom has finally paid off."

"It sounds like such a cool job," Emmy said. "Getting to meet all those musicians and set up concerts."

"Yeah, she loves it. The pay's pretty up and down, though. As soon as the economy takes a hit, nobody wants to go to concerts anymore. She doesn't like to let on, but I think she's been a bit worried lately." He wiped his forehead and pulled the binder closer. "Anyway, we're getting the restaurant gift certificates emailed to us, right?"

"Right," Emmy said, "and I already locked up the paintings in the student conference room. That brings us to almost a hundred items. That should be enough, right?"

"Definitely. How's Lola holding up?"

Emmy groaned. "Don't ask. She's determined to raise more money than last year."

"But that's good, isn't it?"

"I wish it was out of the goodness of her heart," Emmy said, "but I think it's more about beating the girls from Wit House, 'cause they organized it last year."

Sam laughed. "Well, at least that'll mean good money for the White Stone Gate Society."

Emmy smiled. The White Stone Gate Society was a charity in King's Lynn that provided food, counseling, and job placements for people who were struggling. The last few years had been hard on Norfolk, and there were a lot of people who needed extra help.

"Brynn said he was collecting a lot of money from ticket sales," Sam said, "so there should be a lot of people to bid on all the auction items."

Emmy's smile slipped, and Sam tipped his head.

"What is it with you guys and Brynn?" he said. "He said you had some kind of rivalry with each other."

Emmy blinked. She wouldn't exactly call it a rivalry. Not only had Brynn given Jack a hard time when they were in first year, but when he'd found out Emmy knew about the Order, he shoved her into a wall and demanded she tell him everything she knew. But Brynn wasn't their rival. He was just a jerk.

Emmy didn't want to explain all that to Sam, especially all the stuff with Jack. It wasn't her place. "We don't exactly get along."

Sam laughed. "Yeah, that's pretty obvious." He stood up. "See you at the committee meeting tomorrow?"

"Sounds good."

Sam hadn't been gone more than a minute when someone else came and sat in his seat. "You two sure have been spending a lot of time together."

Emmy didn't have to look up. She'd know her old roommate's voice anywhere. "What do you want, Victoria?"

"Can't I just come over to catch up?" She smirked and flicked her blond hair behind her shoulder. "We were so close."

"Oh, please," Emmy scoffed. "Seriously, what do you want?"

"To give you a warning."

Emmy shifted in her chair. If the Order was sending messages through Victoria now, it was starting to get ridiculous. "About what?"

"About Sam."

Emmy laughed. "Are you serious?"

"Yes." Victoria crossed her arms. "Just because you two are getting cozy in the common room doesn't mean you actually know him."

Emmy kept laughing. If this was how Victoria wanted to torture her this year, she'd have to come up with something better.

"Did you know he was kicked out of his last two schools?" Victoria asked.

"Says who?"

"Says his official school record."

Emmy stopped laughing. "What, are you snooping into people's personal files now?"

Victoria shrugged. "If someone that cute shows up, you don't think I'm going to do a little research?"

Emmy rolled her eyes, but her chest felt tight. Had Sam really been kicked out of two different schools?

"And they weren't even independent schools," Victoria said. "He was at *state* schools." She said "state" like it was a slug that had squelched through her garden.

"There's nothing wrong with not going to a private school," Emmy said. Now her jaw was tight, too.

"Maybe," Victoria said, "maybe not...but can you imagine

what he must have done to get chucked out of them? If they kicked out students based on the rules at *our* kind of schools, theirs would be empty."

Our kind of schools. She meant schools for rich kids. "There are plenty of people here on scholarship, you know. And by the way, being rich doesn't make you better than everyone else."

"Don't pretend you live in some shack in America," Victoria sneered. "I know what your mother does for a living."

Emmy didn't say anything. Her mom *did* make a lot of money. She knew how lucky she was and that her mom's money didn't make her better than anyone else.

"Anyway, it had to be pretty serious, don't you think?" Victoria said.

"Are you done?" Emmy glared at Victoria.

She got up and smiled sweetly. "Just trying to be helpful."

Emmy shook her head and stuffed her binder into her bag. She could pretty much guarantee that Victoria would never genuinely try to help her. She was probably just messing with Emmy like usual.

But what if she wasn't? What if she was actually telling the truth? Had Sam really been kicked out of two different schools? He seemed like such a nice guy...

Emmy threw her bag over her shoulder and stomped upstairs. Victoria was probably lying. Probably.

Emmy placed the last gift certificate on the long table at the front of the Hall where the silent auction was set up and ran through the office into the student conference room. She'd forgotten pens, which would make it a lot harder for people to bid for items. Before she could enter her access code, Sam burst out of the room.

"Got the pens," he said. "I printed off some extra auction sheets, just in case some of them get filled up."

"Good idea."

They raced back to the Hall together, shimmying past parents who had arrived early for the charity supper. They squeezed through the oak doors to find Lola running straight toward them.

"Have either of you seen Brynn?" she said.

Emmy looked at Sam, who shook his head. "No, why?"

"Because he's supposed to take all the money from people who haven't paid for their tickets yet," she exploded. "*And* the money for the silent auction, *and* any other donations that come in. He's the bloody treasurer. He needs to be here!"

"Um, Lola?" said a little voice behind them.

Oliver was standing there with a metal box in his hands.

"What?" Lola yelled.

Emmy elbowed her. Oliver looked like he might melt into a puddle of nerves.

Lola took a deep breath. "Sorry, Oli. What do you need?"

"Um, Brynn told me he wasn't feeling very well, and he needs you to do all the money stuff tonight."

Lola's scream echoed off every stone in the giant hall.

"Somebody else has to do it," Lola said. "I've got to keep this whole circus running."

"Sam and I need to stay at the silent auction all night," Emmy said.

Lola looked around. "Where's Jack?"

"He and I are hosting, remember?" Oliver said in a quivering voice. "We have to show people how to find their seats and—"

"Fine." Lola grabbed the box. "This was his plan the whole time. Make sure I get stuck with the hardest job when I already have a million things to do tonight."

"It is for a good cause, you know," Emmy said quietly. She hoped Lola hadn't forgotten why they were doing this. The White Stone Gate Society helped a lot of people, and these kinds of events made a big difference for them.

Lola's face softened. "I know." She rolled her shoulders back and marched toward the door. "Let's make some money."

Emmy and Sam took their places by the silent auction table. They were supposed to answer any questions people had…and make sure no one slipped a gift certificate into their pocket. People started browsing the table and bidding almost right away.

Sam wiggled his eyebrows at Emmy. "Looks like we are going to have a good night."

Emmy felt a familiar rush of heat in her ears. She knew he was talking about the silent auction making good money, but spending the entire evening with Sam felt like a good night to her.

Somebody tapped Emmy on the shoulder. "Well, what do you have to say for yourself?"

Emmy whirled around and her jaw dropped. *Lucy* was staring at her, looking so sour it was like she'd swallowed a lemon.

"Um, sorry, what?" Emmy had no idea that Lucy was even coming to the supper.

"I haven't heard a word from you since you got on the train. How am I supposed to look after you if you're completely ignoring me?"

Now it was Emmy's turn to stare. She'd gotten the definite impression that Lucy had no interest in looking after her. She figured Lucy had pretty much forgotten about her the moment she'd gotten on the train.

"Um…"

"Spit it out, love. I haven't got all night."

"Sorry, I didn't know you wanted me to keep in touch," she mumbled.

"Listen, a little birdie told me you're a much bigger trouble-maker than I thought."

Emmy didn't know what to say. She'd never been called a troublemaker in her life.

"We've been getting questions about you from some people at the Thackery Club. It's causing real trouble for us."

"How would people there even know who I am?"

"Apparently some of them have kids here."

Emmy frowned. That seemed like a pretty big coincidence. Could these people be members of the Order?

"Seems like you have quite the reputation, and I won't have you dragging down *our* reputation with any hijinks this year, do you understand?"

Emmy nodded and tucked her hair behind her ear. She wished Sam wasn't listening to this.

"I want weekly updates on what kinds of marks you're getting and how much you're studying. If you leave school, I want to know where you are at all times, and don't bother lying. I'll be ringing your teachers to check up on you."

Emmy felt her mouth hanging open. Even her mother wouldn't dream of being that strict.

"Have you got all that?" Lucy snapped.

Emmy nodded. She was too shocked to do anything else. Why had she suddenly turned into Emmy's personal dictator?

Lucy spun on her heel and marched back to her table. All Emmy could do was stare.

"She's quite the charmer," Sam said.

"Uh, yeah."

"Is your mum always like that?"

"Oh, that's not my mom," Emmy mumbled. "It's her cousin. My mom's not coming."

"Mine neither," Sam said. "She's got a big concert in London. It's the last major one she has booked for a while, so it has to go off without a hitch."

Emmy looked down and shuffled her feet. She wanted to crawl under a rock. She didn't want to know what Sam thought of her after hearing all that.

"Don't worry about what your cousin said. She seems like a

right piece of work. Besides, I know what it's like to be called a troublemaker."

Emmy didn't look up. If she really admitted it, the things Victoria had said about Sam had been bothering her. She didn't know what was worse—wondering if what Victoria had said was true, or the fact that Victoria had found a way to annoy her yet again.

"Yeah, I heard you had a bit of, um, trouble at some other schools."

Sam tipped his head to one side. "What did you hear?"

Emmy bit her lip. What was it Lola had said the first day they'd met? *If you want to know something about someone, you should just bloody well ask.* She took a few steps away from the table and nodded for Sam to join her.

"Somebody told me that you had been kicked out of a bunch of schools," she blurted out.

Even in the darkly lit Hall, Emmy could see his cheeks going red.

She put her face in her hands. What was she thinking? She had totally embarrassed him. She wished there was a trapdoor under her that would send her into the tunnels. Taking on the Order would be better than this.

"Oh gosh, I'm sorry," she said. "I shouldn't have—"

"No, it's fine." He shook his head. "Wow, word travels fast around here."

Emmy buried her face even deeper. Now he thought she was a gossip.

"Well, your friend didn't get it quite right," Sam said. "It was just one school."

Emmy uncovered her face and tried to ignore her own mortification. "You don't have to tell me. I shouldn't have asked."

"Really, it's okay," Sam said. "I, uh, got into a little trouble with hacking."

"Hacking? Like, computer hacking?"

Sam nodded.

"Oh. I didn't know someone could be expelled for that."

Sam wrinkled his nose. "You can when you hack into school computers and give all your friends better grades."

Emmy burst out laughing and tried to cover her mouth. "Sorry, I shouldn't laugh."

"Don't worry, I laugh about it, too. I'm not sure whether it was the cleverest thing I've ever done or the stupidest, but it's got to be one or the other." Sam ran his hands through his hair. "Mum wasn't too pleased, though. She thought I must have fallen into a bad crowd. That's why she sent me here. She was so excited when my scholarship came through. I think she's

61

hoping I'll find some good male role models or something. She's been sensitive about that since my dad died."

Emmy stopped laughing. "Oh, I'm sorry."

Sam looked down and scuffed his shoe on the floor. "It was a while ago."

"I haven't seen my dad since I was three," Emmy said.

"That sucks." Sam glanced up at her. "Do you ever hear from him or anything?"

"I heard from him a few times last year," Emmy said, "but his letters aren't exactly…um…normal."

Emmy just about clapped her hand over her mouth. What was she thinking, telling Sam she'd heard from her dad? Two minutes of staring into those hazel eyes had made her give up her biggest secret.

She looked around. There were a couple of older ladies at the auction table, but they weren't close enough to have heard. Everybody else was busy finding their seats and talking.

Sam was still looking at her and Emmy cleared her throat.

"It's kind of complicated," she muttered.

"Yeah, I get it." He smiled at her and Emmy felt a warm feeling in her chest. She'd taken a chance on opening up to Jack and Lola last year and it had really paid off. Maybe it was good to let one more person in.

A woman waved at them from the silent auction table. "Excuse me, could I get some help?"

Emmy had almost forgotten that they were supposed to be working. They hurried back to the table and Emmy double-checked to make sure the items were all still there. The last thing they needed was a theft.

Chapter 6

Accusations

The rest of the evening went by fast, and by the time the auction closed, they'd raised almost ten thousand pounds for the White Stone Gate Society. The committee called all the final bidders up to collect their cash and checks, and Lola stuffed everything into the overflowing money box.

"Does anybody know who Brynn arranged to give all the money to?" Lola asked. Everybody shook their heads.

"Can you give it to your mom or Larraby?" Jack asked.

"Mum already left," Lola said. "Her leg was really bothering her, and who knows where Larraby is. I'll just lock it in the student conference room and tell Brynn he has to deal with it tomorrow." She stuffed the money box under her arm. "Don't forget to have all your stuff out of the conference room tonight, 'cause they're going to deactivate our access codes in the morning."

Lola left the Hall quickly. Emmy could tell she was exhausted. She hadn't stopped running around all night.

"I'm going to turn in," Sam said with a yawn.

They said goodnight to him, and Jack dropped into a chair next to Emmy. "I think my hosting duties are finally done." People were drinking the last of their champagne and filing out the doors.

"How did Oliver do?" Emmy couldn't imagine him having to talk to all these strangers.

"Not bad," Jack said. "He's a really good kid, you know. He's just nervous about fitting in."

Emmy smiled wryly. "Kind of like you were when you first started here?"

Jack elbowed her in the ribs. "Hey, you weren't even here then!"

"It's not like it's a secret. I know you had a rough time."

"Yeah. I don't want him to go through that."

"You really care about him, don't you?"

Jack looked down at his hands. "He's my brother. He's not like Malcolm and Vincent. They've always had that swagger, like they know they belong in every room they walk into. But Oli... He's more..."

"Like you?"

"Yeah. I just want him to be okay, you know?"

Emmy smiled. "Yeah, I know."

Jack pushed his chair away from the table. "Anyway, I'm beat. I'm going to grab my stuff and get out of here."

"Me too."

They grabbed their jackets from the student conference room, along with their planning binders and any other things they'd needed for the night. Emmy had liked working on the event, but she was glad it was done. Soccer season was starting soon, and she didn't need anything extra on her plate.

It was a huge relief to get back to Audrey House and into bed. Emmy's feet were killing her. That was the last time she'd borrow shoes from Jaya. She fell asleep almost instantly and didn't wake up until she heard shouting from the common room the next morning.

Emmy rolled out of bed and plodded down the stairs. Lola

and Brynn were facing each other, and Lola looked like she was ready to explode. Brynn seemed as relaxed as ever.

"Obviously you didn't look hard enough!" Lola yelled.

Brynn shrugged. "Come take a look for yourself. Your mum and I searched every drawer and cupboard. The money box isn't there."

One hour later, the entire fund-raising committee was sitting in the student conference room. Emmy, Jack, and Lola were all fidgeting nonstop, while Oliver and Sam just looked confused. They hadn't been in the common room that morning. Oliver kept chewing his lip and looking at his brother, as if Jack could reveal the meeting's secret meaning. The only person who looked totally at ease was Brynn. In fact, he looked downright smug.

"So…does anybody know why Boyd and Larraby hauled us in here?" Sam asked.

"It would appear," Brynn said slowly, "that somebody here is a thief."

Sam and Oliver both shifted in their chairs, but Emmy kept staring at Brynn. She knew exactly who that "somebody" was.

The conference room door opened and Boyd and Larraby

walked in. Ms. Blakely, the new head of security, was with them, along with someone Emmy had rarely seen in a whole year at Wellsworth—Headmaster Haverham. He was short with close-cropped hair, and every time Emmy saw him, he was wearing a perfectly tailored suit. This morning was no exception. He put his briefcase on the table and pulled out a leather binder.

"Good morning," Headmaster Haverham said.

The room chorused "Good morning" back to him.

He cleared his throat. "Good morning, *sir*."

Everyone mumbled "Good morning, sir," even Lola, who must have been too nervous to remember how much she hated being corrected.

"Who was working the silent auction last night?" Haverham asked.

"Sam and I were," Emmy said, her voice cracking a bit.

Haverham looked at her. "What's your name?"

"Emmeline Willick," she responded. This seemed like one of those times that she should use her full name.

"And who is Sam?"

Sam raised his hand. "Sam Corby, sir."

Haverham looked at Sam. "How was the money collected for each item, Mr. Corby?"

"Lola collected all the money and put it in the money box," Sam said.

"Lola Boyd?" the headmaster said quickly, glancing over to where Lola sat.

Sam nodded.

"And how did most people pay?" he asked Lola.

"Most people paid with checks," she said. "A few of the smaller items were cash, though. And a lot of the ticket money was cash."

The headmaster made more notes in his binder, and Emmy bit her lip. It didn't sound like they'd found the money yet.

"And what happened to that box at the end of the night?" he asked.

"I didn't know who Brynn had arranged to take the money." Lola glared at him. "He completely bailed on us last night."

"I wasn't feeling well," Brynn said.

"That's total rubbish," Lola snapped. "You were fine yesterday morning, and you're fine now!"

"Maybe it was something I ate," Brynn said casually. "In any case, I went to get the money this morning, and it was gone."

"That's convenient." Lola folded her arms across her chest. "How do we know you didn't take all that cash and tell us you couldn't find it?"

"Because your mum was with me," Brynn sneered.

Everyone looked at Madam Boyd.

"I was in the office this morning," Boyd said. "Mr. Stratton asked me to open the student conference room, as his code had already been deactivated. We both searched the room, but there was no money box."

Brynn leaned back in his chair and smirked at Lola. "How do we know you didn't take all that cash and tell us you locked it up? Besides, I've got plenty of pocket money; I don't need to steal. You, on the other hand..."

Lola shoved her chair back and sprang to her feet. "If your granddad hadn't cut Mum off, we'd be rolling in it, too!"

"Lola!" her mother barked.

Emmy and Jack yanked Lola back into her chair. The less ammunition she gave Brynn, the better.

"Miss Boyd," the headmaster clipped, "I would advise you to keep your temper in check. For once." His eyes were narrow and harsh. That wasn't a good sign.

"Lola," Madam Boyd said, "tell us exactly what happened when you left the Hall with the money box."

Lola gritted her teeth. "I grabbed the box, went to the loo, and put the box in that drawer." She pointed at a drawer in the cupboard on the wall, never taking her eyes off Brynn.

"You stopped at the lavatory?" the headmaster said.

"Yeah."

"You couldn't have done that after you had locked the money away?"

Lola glared. "I'd been working like mad all night. Do you have any idea how badly I had to pee?"

His jaw went tight, and Ms. Blakely put up her hands. "All right, all right. Miss Boyd, did anyone see you?"

"There were loads of people in the entrance hall," she said. "So yeah, a ton of people saw me."

"Did you stop to talk to anyone? Can anyone confirm how long you were in the bathroom or in the conference room?"

"I don't know, I—"

"I can," Oliver said quietly. Everyone turned to look at him. "I was talking to my dad, and I saw Lola come out of the Hall." He swallowed. "It was just like she said. She went to the loo, went to the conference room, and that was it."

"How long was she in the conference room?" Blakely asked.

"Not long," he said. "Basically just in and out."

"Did you happen to notice how long Miss Boyd was in the lavatory?" Haverham asked.

Oliver shrank back in his chair. "Um, I guess it was kind of a while."

Lola's cheeks went pink. "Well, I mean, some things can't be rushed," she sputtered.

"Of course." The headmaster looked heavily at Madam Boyd, whose knuckles were going white. He straightened his tie and smoothed out his jacket. "I'm afraid we'll need to have a word with Miss Boyd. Everyone else is free to go."

The pink tinge in Lola's cheeks turned to a deep red.

"Can Emmy and I stay behind?" Jack asked Madam Boyd.

She shook her head. "I'm sure we can sort this out." She sounded a lot more confident than she looked.

"I guess this means you haven't found the money?" Emmy asked.

Madam Boyd closed her eyes. "No, we found it."

Emmy frowned and looked back at Lola. She was obviously trying to seem calm, but her shaking fingers were giving her away.

"Now," Larraby said, speaking for the first time, "out you go. I'm sure the full story will hit all the gossip channels soon enough."

Emmy reluctantly walked out into the entrance hall. She wasn't interested in gossip. She was only interested in making sure her best friend was going to be okay.

She and Jack waited outside until the others were gone and then pressed their ears hard against the door.

"Can you hear anything?" Emmy whispered.

He grimaced. "Not really. I think I heard something about cameras."

"Right, the security cameras!" Emmy breathed out. "They'll show Lola didn't take the money, right?"

"There are no cameras in the bathrooms or the conference room," Jack said, "so they wouldn't show anything if she took the money while she was in there."

Emmy smacked his shoulder. "She didn't take the money at all!"

"Ow!" Jack rubbed his shoulder and glared at her. "I know that! But the headmaster doesn't."

Emmy sighed. "What else can you hear?"

Jack pressed his ear to the door again. "I'm not sure. It sounds like Madam Boyd, but I can't make out what she's saying."

They crouched by the door for another half an hour, making out a few words here and there, but never getting much sense of what was going on.

"Is that…?" Emmy's heart sank. "Is somebody crying?"

Jack's eyes were wide. "I think so."

Emmy heard the sound of chairs scraping on the floor. "Quick!" She pulled Jack away from the door, and they launched themselves toward the opposite wall.

The door opened. Headmaster Haverham left first and walked straight into his office and closed the door. Master Larraby came out, shaking his head.

"Shocking business," he muttered to himself.

Finally, out came Lola and her mother, who had wrapped her arms around Lola's shoulders. Lola's eyes were red and bright with tears. Emmy swallowed hard. She'd never seen Lola cry before.

Jack looked like he was ready to cry, too. "What happened?"

Lola took a shuddering breath. "They found the money in my dresser. I'm being expelled."

Chapter 7

Scapegoat

Emmy was sure that her heart had stopped beating. It couldn't be true. Not Lola.

"What are you talking about?" Jack choked out.

"They searched all the committee members' rooms this morning and"—she gulped back a sob—"they found all the cash and checks in my dresser."

"But that's ridiculous!" Emmy said. "Why would you take the money?"

Lola shrugged. "Haverham doesn't care."

"He's got to know you'd never do anything like this," Jack said.

Lola wiped her eyes and Madam Boyd rubbed her shoulder. "He said my record is against me."

Emmy winced. That was true. Lola had punched Brynn in her first year, and then hit a girl during a soccer match a year later.

"Rubbish," Madam Boyd said. Her jaw was tight and her face bright red. "There's a huge difference between losing your temper and creating a plan to steal from a charity."

"But...but where will you go?" Emmy asked.

Lola looked at her mom. It didn't seem like they'd come up with an answer for that yet.

"Come on," Madam Boyd said. "We'd better call your father."

Lola and her mom disappeared into the office, and the knots in Emmy's stomach twisted even tighter. Lola's dad lived in Scotland. Emmy didn't know exactly how far away that was, but she knew it wasn't close. "Lola wouldn't actually have to move back to Glasgow, would she?"

Jack rubbed the bridge of his nose. "Where else is she supposed to go?" He kept rubbing his nose and then finally his eyes as tears started dripping down his face. "I can't lose her, Em. She was my lifeline that first year. I really don't know what I would have done if she hadn't come along. And now…" He wiped his eyes with his sleeve.

Emmy put her arm around him. "We'll figure this out. We won't let her go." She wished she was as brave as she sounded. She couldn't imagine life here without Lola, either.

"We should never have let Brynn be on the committee. We should have known he'd do something horrible." She'd never imagined it would be this horrible, though.

Heat rushed through her body. There was no way she'd let Brynn frame her best friend for something she didn't do. She whirled around and marched down the hallway and across the grounds with Jack trailing behind her. She flung open the Audrey House door and scanned the common room. Brynn wasn't there.

She slammed her hand on the Edmund staircase banister and stomped up the first few steps.

"Whoa," Jack called, "what are you doing?"

"I'm going to find that little weasel."

"And do what?"

Emmy whipped around. "Force him to tell the truth! That he took that money and planted it in her room."

"And how are you going to do that?"

Emmy stopped. She had no idea how she'd force Brynn to confess.

Jack ran his hands through his hair. "If you go up there, you're just going to get in trouble. Brynn will rat you out for being on the boys' side."

Emmy crossed her arms and looked away. She didn't care about getting in trouble right now.

"Look," Jack said, "nothing you say or do to Brynn is going to get him to tell the truth."

"Maybe not, but kicking him would sure make me feel better."

"But it wouldn't help Lola."

She sighed. Jack was right. She couldn't give Brynn even more ways to get them into trouble.

They sat on one of the couches, and Emmy rubbed her legs to try to get them to stop twitching. Maybe when Lola came back, they could go for a run. They'd probably both need it. It was over an hour before Lola came through the door. Her eyes were dry now, but her face was still pale and blotchy.

"Well?" Jack asked quietly.

"Dad's going to ring an estate agent in King's Lynn tomor-row," Lola said dully. "He'll rent out his flat in Glasgow, and since he works from home, he says it's not a big deal for him to move down here, at least for now. Hopefully he'll find a flat right away we can both stay in, and I can start at a state school close by. I'm allowed to stay in my mum's flat until then."

It felt like someone kicked Emmy in the gut. Lola's dad was moving, which meant this was really happening. Unless they could figure out a way to stop it, Lola was going to leave Wellsworth.

Emmy helped Lola pack her things and move them into her mom's apartment in the teacher's housing. Jack came along to help Lola get settled, and by the time they made it back to the house, it was well past curfew. Not that it mattered. Madam Boyd wasn't about to get mad at them for it.

When she finally got to bed, Emmy tossed around more than she slept. By morning, she felt achy and queasy. She just wanted to curl up and cry. She felt like a zombie in her classes, and Jack didn't look much better. Sam seemed to be sticking closer to him than usual and trying to make him laugh. It was nice that Jack had a roommate he could depend on.

When the bell sounded at the end of humanities, all Emmy wanted to do was take a nap.

"Miss Willick?" Master Barlowe was standing beside the row she was sitting in. "Do you mind if we have a word?"

Emmy nodded and trudged down the stairs in the giant lecture hall. Barlowe's desk sat in a corner of the round platform at the bottom of the stairs. He waited at the door until everyone was gone, closed it, and ambled down the staircase.

"I heard about Miss Boyd," he said. "I'm so sorry, Emmy."

Emmy nodded again. She was too tired to be angry right now.

"Obviously you believe that she's innocent?"

"Yes," she said firmly.

Barlowe put his hands in his pockets and leaned against his desk. "Do you know who the real culprit might—"

"It was Brynn."

"You're sure?"

"Positive."

He slowly paced across the platform, his shoes clicking on the old hardwood. "Do you have any idea why he'd want to frame her?"

"Because he hates her," she said immediately. "He hates all three of us."

"And you don't think there might have been another

reason?" Barlowe stopped walking and looked at her. "That he might have been doing it on someone else's instructions?"

Emmy blinked. He was talking about the Order, but why would they come after her now? They couldn't possibly know what she'd put in that safe-deposit box in London. Could they?

"I don't have anything they want," Emmy said. "Besides, the Order doesn't have any reason to go after Lola."

Barlowe pressed his lips together. "Sometimes going after a loved one is…more effective."

Something icy crept up her spine. "I don't have anything they want," she repeated, but a little quieter this time.

Barlowe leaned against his desk again and looked at his shoes. "Is it possible that some of the items that you lost… weren't actually lost?"

Emmy shuffled her feet. Other than Jack and Lola, she hadn't told a single soul that she still had the medallions, and she wasn't about to start telling now. "It's not possible."

"Have you heard about the Latin Society's latest project?"

She shook her head.

"They say they found evidence of Roman ruins on the cliffs near the round tower church. They've sponsored an archaeological dig to see if there are any remains off-shore."

"I'm sure anything that went into the sea there is long gone," she said truthfully. All she'd tossed in there was a cardboard box. That wouldn't have survived long.

"As it happens, that area was already searched by divers." Barlowe looked at her. "We didn't find anything, either."

Emmy chewed on the inside of her cheek. Barlowe and her dad were just as focused on those medallions as Jonas was, but for different reasons. Barlowe had helped her last year, but what if that was more about the medallions than it was about her? As for her dad... Well, his life hadn't been about Emmy for a long time.

"If my dad wants those medallions so badly, why did he leave them in our house in Connecticut?" she asked. "Or why didn't he come back for them when they were just sitting there for ten years? Shouldn't he have broken into those vaults ages ago and, like, donated everything to a museum or something so the Order would never have it?"

"It's not that simple." Barlowe glanced at the door at the top of the stairs and took a few steps toward her. "Those vaults were built deep under the abbey more than five hundred years ago. Everyone used to think they were just a legend. No one in the Order took them seriously. In his last year of school, your father started doing significant research about the Order and its history, and he discovered that the vaults were real. Figuring out where they are is a different matter."

Emmy blinked. "Are you saying nobody actually knows where the vaults are?"

"I can't say for sure," Barlowe said. "The research your father did suggests that at one time there was a way to get to them without even using medallions, but there have been cave-ins over the years and some of the oldest tunnels are blocked. Given how desperately the Order has been searching for those medallions, we believe they have found a way to get through using the locked passageways. If Jonas thinks you still have some of the medallions, getting Lola kicked out might be the first step in trying to get you to hand them over."

"He's the one who saw them fly into the sea," Emmy whispered. "He knows they're gone." At least she hoped he did. "And why would he be doing this expedition thing if he thinks I still have them?"

"I don't know, but I find it hard to believe that Brynn is going after Lola just because he doesn't like her. There has to be more going on here." Barlowe pressed his fingers to his lips. "If you find out anything else, or if the situation changes, please tell me."

"Okay," Emmy said, even though she wasn't sure if she

actually would. She wasn't sure of much anymore. She started up the first few steps.

"By the way," Barlowe said, "have you met Ms. Blakely yet?"

"Um, yeah." Emmy bit her lip. "Do you know if she's part of—"

"I can't imagine that she would be," Barlowe said. "I heard Larraby telling her about a little club that he sponsors, and how they use a couple of old passageways. A lot of teachers know of the Order that way." He smiled. "I don't think you have anything to fear from her."

Emmy nodded. At least that was one person she didn't have to worry about.

Emmy and Jack visited Lola every day after school that week. Figuring out how they could prove Lola was innocent was pretty much the only thing they talked about. By Friday, they still didn't have any viable ideas.

Lola was having dinner with her mom, so Emmy and Jack went back early that night.

"Want to play a game with me and Sam?" Jack offered as they walked back from having a somber dinner in the Hall.

"Thanks, but I think I'm going to turn in early." Once they got to the common room, Emmy waved goodnight to Jack, walked upstairs, rummaged under her blankets, and found her pajamas. She just wanted to curl up and watch something on her laptop. She grabbed it off the desk and was about to pull it onto the bed when something fell off the top of it. It was a USB drive that had her name taped to the side.

Emmy frowned. That wasn't hers. At least, she was pretty sure it wasn't. Maybe someone had found it in her old room and assumed it must have belonged to her, or maybe she'd lost it so long ago that she'd forgotten. She plugged it into her laptop and found only one item in the folder: a video labeled WHO FRAMED LOLA BOYD?

Emmy's heart thudded in her chest as she clicked on the video file. When it opened, she froze.

Jonas Tresham was staring at her.

She clicked the play button with a shaky finger, and Jonas started to speak.

"Good evening, young miss."

A nasty taste flooded Emmy's mouth. The last time she'd heard that voice, it had been threatening to kill her.

"I'm sorry that your friend Lola has been expelled from

Wellsworth. Rest assured, she will be proved innocent and reinstated as soon as possible."

Emmy narrowed her eyes. There was no way Jonas would do that without wanting something in return.

"Before I can make those arrangements, I'll need some information from you. We recently received proof that your father is alive and well."

Emmy's stomach dropped. Her dad had always been so careful. How could they have found him now?

"We don't know where he is at the moment," Jonas went on, "but you can help us with that. Tell us where he is, and Lola will be back in her room the next day."

Emmy almost laughed out loud. Did Jonas really think she'd hand her father over to the Order? No way. She and Jack would just have to clear Lola's name on their own.

"Of course, if we don't get the information we need from you, we'll have to, shall we say, press our point a little harder."

Emmy felt the blood drain from her face.

"Tell us where your father is, or your friend will get far worse than expulsion." Jonas's tone was so matter-of-fact it was like he was sending Emmy a casual greeting instead of a threat.

"In case you're thinking of sharing this file, you should know that it's set to self-delete sixty seconds after being opened."

Emmy checked the video length; it was fifty-five seconds. There's no way she'd be able to make a copy in time.

"I look forward to hearing from you soon."

The video stopped. Then the image fractured and disappeared. The file folder was empty.

Chapter 8

The Usual Suspects

Emmy pressed two shaking fingers to her lips. Somebody from the Order had been in her room. The dorm rooms didn't have locks—someone had told her that they used to, but people kept locking themselves out, so they were finally removed. Still, nobody ever seemed to violate the unwritten rule of never going in someone's room without permission.

She pulled her blanket around her shoulders. Could it have been Brynn? He'd already apparently been in Lola's room, so he obviously didn't care much about that rule. Maybe he'd gotten a girl to do it for him. Victoria wouldn't pass up a chance to mess with her, even if she didn't know anything about the Order. She might have put the money in Lola's room, too. She'd probably be giddy at the chance to get Lola kicked out.

Emmy barely slept that night. Even the sound of Natalie's white noise machine couldn't lull her to sleep. The Order was after her again. Except they weren't. They were after her friend, and that felt ten times worse.

At breakfast, she grabbed some dry toast and was about to slump into a chair next to Jack when Victoria walked past.

"Did you have a nice night?" Emmy asked her.

Victoria blinked. "Why are you talking to me?"

"I was just wondering how your evening was. Did you do anything fun?"

Victoria looked around like she was checking to make sure she hadn't entered some kind of alternate universe.

"Like maybe breaking into somebody's room and leaving them a message?"

Jack shifted in his chair, and Victoria just shook her head.

"So, you've finally cracked," Victoria said. "It was only a matter of time before you completely lost it." She didn't seem to be covering up any guilt. She just seemed totally confused.

Emmy shrugged. "Never mind." She sat next to Jack and Victoria left, whispering to one of her friends. It didn't really matter if Victoria had been the one to put the USB drive in her room, or if she had hidden the money box. Brynn was the one who was really behind it.

"Something going on?" Jack asked.

Emmy glanced at Oliver, who was sitting in the next chair. "Later," she muttered.

Oliver didn't look too happy, either. He just kept pushing his sausage around his plate or swirling it in his baked beans.

"What about you, Oli? Everything okay?" Jack asked.

"I guess." He bit his lip. "I'm really sorry about Lola. I can't believe she's being expelled." He looked like he was ready to cry.

"Don't worry," Jack said. "We'll get her off. She'll be back in class in no time." He smiled unconvincingly.

Oli nodded weakly.

Jack cleared his throat. "Tell us more about your first few weeks. Have you met some good people? Do you like your teachers?"

Oliver shrugged.

Jack and Emmy looked at each other. Oliver didn't seem to be having a good time at school.

"What about societies?" Jack said. "Have you joined any?"

"Just Latin."

Jack dropped his fork. "Why'd you join them?" he asked a bit too loudly.

"Dad told me to," Oliver muttered.

Emmy pressed her lips together. If Mr. Galt wanted Oliver to join Latin Society, he must be planning to have Oli in the Order. Emmy didn't know what Oliver knew about the Order. Jack had known quite a bit when Emmy had met him, but he had been older. And Oli was pretty unassuming—it seemed like he could be pushed around pretty easily. Those kinds of kids often didn't do so well with the boisterous, sometimes rebellious Latin Society boys. As a matter of fact, a boy like that had fallen off a roof during a stunt the year before.

"So, um, what do you think of it so far?" Emmy gently prodded.

"It's all right, I guess."

Jack wiped his face with a napkin, like he was giving himself time to think. "Listen, both Emmy and I have been in Latin Society, and, well, it didn't turn out great for either of us."

"Really? Why not?"

Jack and Emmy looked at each other again. They didn't want to give Oliver too many details, especially about the Order.

"They can be a bit of a rough crowd," Jack said. "They tend to get younger kids into a lot of trouble. I really, really think you shouldn't go."

Oliver looked down at his plate. "Well, Dad really wants me to, so..."

"Sometimes Dad is... Well, you know what he's like."

Oliver sniffed.

"If the only reason you're going is to impress Dad, then being in that society isn't going to go well." Jack ducked his head down so he could look Oli in the eye. "You need to do your own thing, you know?"

Oliver nodded, but he didn't seem too sure. Jack looked like he wanted to say more but he didn't know what. Finally, he went back to eating his porridge.

Since it was Saturday, Emmy and Jack went straight to Madam Boyd's apartment after breakfast. They had just about reached the door when Emmy's cell phone rang.

"Hello?"

"Oh, so your phone does work," said a snarky voice.

"Um, who is this?"

"It's Lucy, and I thought you agreed to tell me if you got into any trouble."

"I'm not in trouble."

"I hear your best friend just got herself chucked out!"

Emmy frowned. "How did you hear about that?"

"Ah, so you admit you were trying to keep it from me."

"What? No. I mean, I'm not the one in trouble," Emmy said, "so why would I—"

"Because you're clearly running with a disreputable crowd," Lucy said. "Your friend has a bad reputation, which means you have a bad reputation, and that reflects very poorly on me."

Emmy shook her head. This conversation didn't make any sense. "How does it reflect poorly on you?" She'd only spent six days with Lucy, and even then, they'd barely spoken to each other.

"Somebody at the Thackery Club is telling everyone that you're *completely* out of control and that we must be doing a terrible job of looking after you. People are starting to question whether we should be admitted to the club."

Someone from the Order must be spreading rumors about Emmy. But why?

"Being offered membership in the Thackery Club means we're back to the top of London's social scene," Lucy said. "That means Harold gets more clients, I get more buyers for my dogs, and we can get a holiday house in Majorca again. Do you have any idea how hard we've had to work since…"

"Since what?"

Lucy seemed to be trying to decide if she should say more. "It doesn't matter," she finally snapped. "What matters is that we're back, and I won't have you jeopardizing that. I want daily updates on your activities—where you are, who you're with, what you're doing. And you are not to see this girl again."

"Sorry," Emmy said quietly. "I'll let you know where I am, but I'm not going to stop seeing my friend."

"Now you listen to me, child. I am in charge of you, and—"

"I can't talk anymore," Emmy said. "I have somewhere to be." She hung up the phone.

"Who was that?" Jack asked.

"Lucy," Emmy said, "going on about her precious Thackery Club."

"I think my parents are members there," Jack said.

Emmy stuffed her phone into her pocket. So, there *were* Order members there. She couldn't worry about it now, though. She had bigger problems than Lucy's reputation.

Jack pressed the button next to Madam Boyd's name and the door buzzed open.

"What took you so long?" Lola asked. "I've been waiting all morning."

Jack looked at his watch. "It's not even ten."

Lola mumbled something and threw herself down on her blanket and pillow, which were still laid out on the couch. The coffee table was littered with chip bags and soccer magazines.

"How are you holding up?" Emmy asked, eyeing the mess.

Lola glared at her and shoved a handful of chips into her mouth.

"Did your dad find a flat?" Jack asked.

Lola swallowed and wiped her mouth with her sleeve. "Yup. He's moving down next weekend so I can start at Erindale on Monday."

"Erindale?" Emmy asked.

"Erindale Academy," Lola grumbled. "My new school."

"Oh." Emmy cleared her throat. "Do you know anything about it?"

"I know their uniforms are dull and their football team's rubbish."

Emmy cringed. She remembered playing Erindale in a couple matches the year before. Lola was right; they weren't very good.

"I guess you'll have no trouble making the team, then," Jack said with an awkward laugh.

"There's no way I'm going to that school," Lola said. "We've got to prove Brynn's guilty by the end of the week, or I'll be stuck playing with a bunch of first years who don't know the difference between their left and right wingers."

Emmy bit her lip. "We might have bigger problems than Brynn."

"What do you mean?" Jack asked.

"I got a message last night. From Jonas."

Jack sprang off the arm of the couch and almost knocked over a lamp. "Jonas?"

"What the bloody hell did he want?" Lola asked.

"He wants my dad." Emmy sank into a tatty armchair and told them about the video.

"He's off his rocker," Lola said. "Does he really think you'd hand your own dad over to a bunch of murderers just so I can go back to school?"

Emmy pressed her lips together. She hadn't told them that Jonas had said worse things were coming, but if they could get Lola back into Wellsworth, she and Jack could make sure Lola was safe while Emmy figured out what to do about Jonas.

"We should probably tell your mum that it's the Order that's framing you," Jack said to Lola.

She gaped at him. "Are you out of your mind? She'd go barmy if she knew they were involved. She'd watch all of us like a hawk to make sure we weren't snooping around, and then we'd never get me out of this mess." She narrowed her eyes at Jack. "You're not going to chicken out and blab, are you?"

"No!" Jack looked a little uncertain, though. His dad and older brothers were all part of the Order, and he knew first-hand what they were capable of.

"Even if the Order's involved," Lola said, "it must have been Brynn who actually took the money. I still think we need to focus on him."

"What if somebody else from the Order took it?" Emmy asked.

"Can't be," Lola said. "Only committee members had the access code."

"And teachers," Jack added. "It could have been Larraby. Or Brynn could have given the code to somebody else. But how do we get proof?"

Lola's shoulders slumped and Emmy looked away. That was the question they'd been talking about all week, and they weren't any closer to finding an answer.

When Emmy and Jack got back to the common room, they found Sam typing on his computer.

"What are you working on?" Jack asked half-heartedly.

"I'm putting up an ad in the student web forums," Sam said, "asking if anybody needs help with tech stuff."

"That's cool," Jack said. "I bet loads of people could use some extra help."

"Yeah, hopefully it'll bring in some extra cash." He closed his laptop. "How's Lola?"

A warm feeling spread through Emmy. Sam seemed genuinely concerned about Lola, which made her like him even more.

"She's getting pretty fed up," Emmy said.

"You're sure it wasn't her, right?" Sam asked.

"Positive," Jack said. "This whole thing's completely nuts."

Sam put his book down and leaned forward. "Any idea who did it?"

Emmy looked at Jack. Telling Sam about the Order probably wasn't a good idea. Then again, they didn't have to mention the Order to talk about who framed Lola.

"Come on." Emmy stood up and nodded toward the door. "Let's go for a walk."

The sun was already getting lower in the sky, giving the forest a faint glow.

"Wow, you guys really don't want to be overheard," Sam said as he followed them deeper into the forest.

"Just a precaution." Emmy tried to sound casual, like keeping away from listening ears was something every twelve-year-old did.

Once Audrey House was out of sight, Emmy and Jack turned around and faced Sam.

"So?" he asked as he glanced around the dark forest nervously.

"It was Brynn Stratton," Emmy said.

Sam raised his eyebrows. "You're sure?"

"Positive," Jack said.

"Isn't he, like, completely minted?"

Emmy blinked. "Huh?"

"He means rich," Jack said.

"Oh, yeah," Emmy said, "definitely minted."

Sam and Jack looked at each other and smiled.

"What?" Emmy asked.

"Sorry," Sam said, "it just doesn't sound right with an American accent."

Emmy rolled her eyes. "Anyway, yeah, he's rich, but he and Lola can't stand each other. He'd do practically anything to get her expelled. We need to find proof that somebody went into the conference room, somebody who shouldn't have been there."

"What about the security footage?" Sam asked.

"Haverham said he looked at it," Jack said.

"Maybe they missed something," Emmy said.

"How can you miss something on a video?" Jack asked.

"Actually, it happens all the time," Sam said. "That kind of footage is usually pretty grainy, so they might not be able to tell one kid in a uniform from another."

"But *we* might be able to," Emmy said. "I bet we can recognize each other better than the headmaster can."

"So how do we get our hands on that footage?" Jack asked.

Sam cleared his throat. "Sounds like you need some help. From someone who has a certain, shall we say, technical know-how. And maybe even some experience with hacking." He grinned.

Emmy looked at Jack. For the first time in a week, he had a glint of hope in his eyes.

"*If* you were to try to get that security footage," Jack said slowly, "what would you do?"

"I couldn't do it remotely because it would already have been archived," Sam said. "I'd have to actually be in the security office and download it onto a drive. So, I'd need a plan to get me in there."

Jack grinned. "Now that's something we can help *you* with."

Chapter 9

A False Sense of Security

Nobody said anything as Emmy, Sam, and Jack made their way down to the basement. They all knew what they were supposed to do. It was a relief for Emmy to not have to hide her nerves during one of their schemes. The more nervous she looked, the better her chances of convincing Ms. Blakely to leave her office. At least…that was the idea.

Emmy had only been down this corridor once before. That was when Jonas had caught them breaking into the school office in the middle of the night. The lights were on down here now, which made it a lot less intimidating. They stopped in front of the door that read "Security."

"Ready?" Jack asked. Sam and Emmy both nodded, and Jack knocked on the door.

Emmy held her breath. Ms. Blakely might not even be in the office right now. The sound of movement inside settled her stomach a little. At least one part of the scheme was going according to plan.

The door opened. "Yes?" Ms. Blakely asked.

The three of them looked at each other nervously.

"Is something wrong?"

"We overheard something," Jack said. He ducked his head and shifted his body like he was uncomfortable but ended up blocking Ms. Blakely's view of the door. "A couple of people were talking about meeting at four thirty for a fight."

Sam slowly reached behind Jack and stuffed a chewed-up piece of gum into the door catch.

"They seemed pretty serious," Jack said. "They were really revved up."

"Did they say where they were going to meet?"

Jack shook his head. "Most fights happen on the cliffs behind the football pitch. I'm sure that's where they'd go."

Ms. Blakely checked her watch. "It'll take at least fifteen minutes to walk there. Let's get a move on." She pushed past them, and the door closed behind her.

Emmy heard the automatic lock try to engage, but it sounded like it stopped partway through. "I'm staying here," she said over the sound of the lock. "I don't want to see a fight."

Ms. Blakely didn't seem to care who went with her. She was already heading for the staircase with Jack trailing behind her. He didn't look back. His part of the plan was mostly done.

Emmy and Sam waited until the footsteps on the stairs faded away, then pushed on the door. It opened. Sam raced into the room while Emmy fished the gum out of the door catch. She tried not to think about how slimy it was as she peeled it off her fingers and into a nearby garbage bin.

"Check for cameras," Sam said. He was already sitting at a long, rounded desk covered with computer monitors.

Emmy looked in each corner of the room. "I don't think there are any in here."

Sam nodded and started tapping on the computer keyboard. "It's asking me for a password."

Emmy typed in the password that Lola had seen her mom

use on other computers. *Please let it still work*. The nearest monitor flickered, and the security camera footage was replaced by a home screen.

"Yes!" Emmy whispered. "Now, how do we find the right footage?"

Sam scanned a list of programs and clicked on one called Blind Eye. The camera footage from the other monitors appeared on the screen, each in a different quadrant. Sam scanned through all the menus so fast Emmy couldn't keep up.

"Have you used this program before?" Emmy asked.

"Nope."

Emmy shook her head. Thank goodness they had Sam. It would have taken her all day to figure this out.

"There's the archive," he said after a few minutes, and a long list of dates appeared. He clicked on the date of the fund-raiser and scrolled until he found a file labeled OFFICE. He stuck a USB drive in the computer, transferred the file, and stuffed it back into his pocket.

"Let's go." Emmy raced toward the door.

"Hang on," Sam said. He clicked on one of the quadrants and scrolled through different camera footage.

"What are you doing?" Emmy asked.

"Causing the camera in this hallway to malfunction," he

said. "It should look like a random failure, but then she won't be able to see us going in and out of here."

Emmy checked her watch. Jack and Ms. Blakely should have made it to the cliffs by now, where they wouldn't find anybody fighting, which meant they were on their way back. They were almost out of time.

Sam was still furiously typing. Emmy kept checking the door. They had to get out.

"Sam, if they find us in here it won't matter if that camera doesn't—"

"Got it," he said. One of the quadrants went black. He put the computer back in sleep mode and they both raced out the door and up the stairs. The upstairs corridors were crowded with people, most of whom had just left a society meeting or were on their way to dinner. Sam and Emmy wove through the crowd and hurried back to Audrey House in silence.

When they got to the common room, Jack was waiting for them.

"Well?" he asked.

"Piece of cake," Sam said. "You?"

"No problem," Jack said with a grin. "Ms. Blakely assumed they must have either chickened out or found some other part of the grounds. She didn't suspect a thing."

Relief washed over Emmy. She leaned over and put her hands on her knees. Her breathing still wasn't back to normal.

"You okay?" Sam asked.

"Yeah," she said in between deep breaths.

Jack shook his head. "You're out of practice. Sneaking around should be old hat to you by now."

"I'm going to start looking through the footage," Sam said. "I can fast-forward through most of it, so it shouldn't take too long. We just need to get a close look at each person who went in there."

"I'll come with you," Jack said.

Sam clapped his hand on Jack's shoulder. "Great!"

They went upstairs and Emmy looked around the common room. Most people were already at dinner, so it was really quiet. She didn't really know what to do next. Usually if Jack was busy, Emmy always had Lola. A deep emptiness settled inside her. She could probably find someone else to sit with at dinner, like maybe Natalie and Jaya. But Natalie and Jaya were best friends, and even though Emmy liked being with them, she'd always be the third wheel.

"Um, Emmy?" said a small voice from behind her.

Emmy turned and saw Oliver sitting at a table a few feet away.

"Hey, Oli."

He had his hands behind his back and looked like he was twisting his fingers together. "Um, I'm having a bit of trouble figuring out this Greek verb conjugation. Do you think you could help me?"

Emmy smiled. "Sorry, I never took first-year Greek. I just did Latin."

His face fell. He looked ready to cry again.

"Oli, are you having some trouble in school?"

He blinked and tears started spilling onto his cheeks. "It's so much harder than my last school, and the other boys…" He wiped his face furiously with his sleeves.

"It's only been a month," Emmy said. "It took me a while to get to know people, too."

He nodded, but Emmy could tell he didn't really believe her.

"Your brother had a lot of trouble in his first year, too," Emmy said. "You should talk to him about it."

Oliver flipped a few pages in his Greek book but didn't say anything. Emmy wasn't sure what to say, either. She really didn't know Oliver that well.

"Come on," Emmy said. "Let's get some dinner."

"You want me to sit with you? Like, just you?" Oliver's

eyes went wide, as if the idea of sitting alone with a fourth-year girl was both magical and terrifying.

"Why not? You're my best friend's brother." She stood up and grinned. "Besides, I bet you'll get way more street cred from the other first years if you have a friend in fourth year."

He quickly ducked his head and stuffed his things in his bag. "Okay."

Emmy smiled and they walked toward the Hall. If she couldn't be with her friends, at least she could help Oliver make some of his own.

By the time Emmy and Oliver came back to the common room, dinner was almost over and Sam and Jack had never shown up.

"Go knock on your brother's door and tell him he'd better hurry if he doesn't want to starve tonight," Emmy told Oliver.

She checked her watch. Study session was going to start in fifteen minutes. She grabbed her English literature textbook and binder from her room and was just setting up a work space when Sam and Jack came flying down the Edmund stairs.

"I'll bring plates back for both of us," Sam said as he ran out the door.

"Finally realized what time it is?" Emmy asked Jack.

"More like we finally finished getting through all the footage," Jack said as he sank into the chair beside her.

"Already?" Emmy sat up straighter.

"Yeah, it didn't take long once we fast-forwarded all the times when there was no one in the office."

Emmy looked around the room. Brynn was nowhere in sight, and the music and talking was so loud it'd be almost impossible to overhear them. "What did you find?"

Jack gave a huge sigh. "Nothing."

"Nothing?" The excitement that had flared in her chest disappeared as quickly as it had come. "What do you mean, nothing?"

"We saw Lola go into the conference room with the box. After she came out, we didn't see anyone unexpected go in there. As far as we could tell, everyone who went in was a committee member, and Brynn didn't go in until he was with Boyd in the morning."

Emmy's insides deflated like an old balloon. "But that means it has to have been a committee member."

113

"How can it be? That's just me, you, Lola, Sam, and Oliver. There's no reason for Oliver to do it, and he'd wet his knickers if he ever got involved in some kind of plot."

"That just leaves Sam." Emmy chewed on the end of her thumb. "You are sure about him, right?" *Please say yes.*

"Definitely," Jack said. "He left early, remember? He was already in his pajamas when I got to our room. The cameras showed you and me going into the conference room only a few minutes after Lola. There's no way he could have grabbed the box, hidden it, gotten out of his dress clothes and into pajamas in that kind of time. Besides, if he had done it, he wouldn't have helped us get that camera footage, not when it points to him as a possible suspect."

Emmy breathed out and nodded. She hadn't really thought it could be Sam. Still, it was nice to have pretty solid proof. "So, what do we do now?"

Jack ran his fingers through his hair. "Well, there were a lot of people in and out of the main office that night. We couldn't always see the student conference room door when the office was really busy, so it's possible somebody could have gotten in without us seeing."

Hope flickered in Emmy's chest. Anything that led away from her friends being suspects was a good thing.

"Could you tell who any of the adults or other students were in the main office?" Emmy asked.

Jack shook his head.

Emmy leaned her chin on her hand. This would have been a great time for her dad to write some letter that magically pointed them in the right direction. But other than asking her for the medallions, she hadn't heard a peep from him in months. Maybe without the medallions, she wasn't really worth his time.

Emmy rubbed her face and sighed. It looked like they were back to square one.

Chapter 10

The Spy

After study session that night, Emmy pulled out her phone and clicked on Lola's name to text her.

We didn't find anything on the security footage.

It was a few minutes before Lola texted back.

That sucks.

Emmy bit her lip.

We'll figure something else out.

I'm moving in three days, Emmy. I don't think Brynn's going to suddenly decide to confess before then.

Fear gnawed at Emmy's stomach. What if they couldn't figure something out? What if Lola really was moving to King's Lynn and there was nothing they could do to stop it?

But there was something. If she found out where her father was, she could tell Jonas. He'd get Lola off the hook, and things would go back to normal. Except they wouldn't, and she knew she couldn't do it.

Emmy rubbed her forehead. She still didn't get how Jonas had figured out her dad had contacted her. Maybe if he hadn't, this never would have happened…and Lola wouldn't be so scared.

I'm not giving up, Lola.

Lola didn't send a message back.

"So, what's next?" Sam said through a mouthful of mashed potatoes the next night.

With a full day of classes and the club she'd just joined (the Medieval Society) after school, she hadn't had to time think about what they might do next. Every day that passed made the panicky feeling in her stomach even stronger. "You're sure you couldn't tell who anybody else was on the security footage?"

"We saw the headmaster go into his office a couple times," Jack said. "That's about it."

Emmy tapped her fork on her plate. "There's no, um"— she glanced at Sam—"no *other* way into the conference room, is there?" She looked at Jack meaningfully. So far, they hadn't told Sam about the Order or any of the tunnels under the school. They really liked him, and they were glad he wanted to help, but they both agreed it was too risky to tell anyone about the Order.

"I guess there could be," Jack said slowly.

"Another way?" Sam asked. "Like, with a hidden door or something?"

Emmy shrugged. "Who knows?"

"But we'd have no way of knowing if somebody got in another way," Jack said.

Emmy's shoulders slumped. Jack was right.

"You still think it was Brynn who masterminded this whole thing, right?" Sam asked.

"Definitely," Emmy said.

"Then we need to get him to talk," Sam said like it was nothing.

Emmy just about spit her milk across the table. "Not going to happen."

"Why not?"

"Brynn's very, very good at keeping secrets," Jack said. "Like, *really* good. Mafia-level good."

"So, you'd need somebody to get close to him, then," Sam said.

"Yeah right." Emmy wiped the milk off her lips and laughed. "Who could we get to do that?"

Sam took a sip of water and grinned. "Me."

Emmy and Jack laughed even louder.

"There is no way he'd fall for that," Jack said.

"He knows you're friends with us," Emmy said. "He'd know for sure that it was a setup."

"We haven't been friends that long," Sam said. "I bet I could sell him on it, especially with all the rumors flying around about me getting kicked out of my last school."

Jack looked at Emmy. He was obviously as skeptical as she was.

"Look, we've hit a dead end," Sam said. "What do we have to lose?"

Jack and Emmy kept looking at each other. Sam had a point. Lola was already moving her things into her dad's new place, and they'd run out of options.

"You could start by going to Latin Society," Jack said. "You might be able to figure out what Larraby's up to as well as Brynn."

"Larraby?" Sam blinked. "What does Master Larraby have to do with anything?"

"Um..." Jack bit his lip and Emmy resisted the urge to groan. How were they supposed to explain why Larraby would be involved without explaining the Order?

"We both had a bit of trouble with Larraby when we were in Latin Society," Emmy said. "He's not... Well, obviously you know he's not great with students."

"He definitely has favorites," Sam said.

"Right," Jack said, "and with Oliver in Latin Society this year, I just want to make sure Larraby doesn't, you know, leave Oli out."

Sam nodded. "I can definitely keep an eye on the old man and on your brother."

Jack looked relieved, and Emmy wasn't sure if it was because he'd managed to cover up his slip about Larraby, or because Sam would genuinely be looking out for Oliver.

"And going to Latin Society should give me plenty of extra time to get Brynn on my side," Sam said.

"It's not like you'd be able to convince him in a day," Jack said. "It might take you all year to gain his trust."

"We can keep trying other things, too."

"There couldn't be a *we* anymore," Emmy said. "If he suspected we were still friends, he'd never let you near him."

"We can create some kind of blowout," Sam said. "And it's not like we can get our rooms reassigned, so Jack and I will still be roommates. That'll give us plenty of time to plan without Brynn ever knowing."

Jack drummed his fingers on the table. "So, what kind of blowout are we talking about?"

The table went quiet. Then Emmy started to smile. "I think I have an idea, but it would involve being a pretty big jerk. Are you up for that?"

Sam grinned. "Always."

Sam started going to Latin Society on Monday. That was the day Lola officially started at her new school. As soon as classes were done, Emmy ripped her phone out of her bag and started texting.

How was your first day?

Lola replied a few moments later.

Like being on a ferris wheel without a seat belt.

Does that mean it was exciting?

It means it was vomit worthy.

Emmy cringed.

Did you find out about soccer trials?

Next week.

You'll probably make some friends on the team.

Lola didn't reply.

Seriously, it's just your first day. Don't freak out yet.

Freaking out is one of my specialties.

Then Lola sent a gif of someone ripping her own hair out.

Emmy laughed.

Relax. It'll be okay.

A few minutes later Lola responded.

Can you spend the weekend in King's Lynn?

I'd have to get permission from my head of house. She's a real taskmaster.

I'll tell her you said that.

Emmy counted down the days until Friday. Not only had Madam Boyd agreed to let Emmy and Jack go, she'd volunteered to drive them. She seemed pretty anxious to see Lola, too.

Emmy had soccer tryouts right after school, so they couldn't leave until the evening. She had a hard time focusing. She missed a couple of simple plays, and she wished Lola was there to yell at her. She managed to do well enough to keep her spot, and by the end of the afternoon, they had two new starters and a couple of reserve players to replace the girls who had left. Lola's replacement was decent enough, but she didn't bring the same kind of energy to the pitch.

Once she had gotten changed, Emmy raced to the parking lot where Jack and Madam Boyd were waiting for her. The drive to King's Lynn took less than an hour, which gave Emmy plenty of time to send Lucy her weekly update. Lucy responded back with a lecture about schoolwork, which Emmy ignored. After a few minutes of driving through town, Madam Boyd pulled her rickety old car into a tiny parking spot. She kicked a few empty beer cans out of the way and led Emmy to a brick courtyard with two or three doors on every wall. She had barely touched the buzzer when someone thundered down the steps inside and flung the door open. Lola flew past her mum and threw herself on Emmy and Jack.

"Bloody hell," Lola said, "thank the freaking stars you're here. I've been stark raving all week!"

Madam Boyd cleared her throat.

"Oh, hi Mum." Lola gave her mom a quick squeeze. "Dad's at the pub. Do you think you could make us something for supper?"

Madam Boyd glared at her. "Of course. There's nothing I love better than cooking in your father's kitchen. That's why we're still married, you know."

Lola rolled her eyes. "There are no groceries, so if you want something better than frozen chips, you'd better find a Tesco's."

"Fine. But you get to spend all weekend with your friends and I only get you for tonight, so be prepared for me to butt in later."

"No problem," Emmy said quickly.

Madam Boyd went back to the car, and Lola led Emmy and Jack up a narrow flight of stairs and through another door.

"Well, this is it," Lola said.

The apartment was tiny, but bright. Lola led them past the little corner kitchen and into a room, which was unmistakably Lola's. Her Rangers F.C. banner hung over a bed littered with clothes and magazines, and there wasn't a single school book in sight.

"So, what's this week really been like?" Jack asked.

Lola flopped down on the bed. "Total rubbish. A couple

of girls recognized me from football, and they've managed to turn half the school against me."

"What?" Emmy sat down beside her. "Why?"

Lola shrugged. "Who knows? They seem to think I'd be all full of myself of something, and that I need to be taken down a peg."

"What are they doing?"

"Just stupid stuff. Saying, 'there's the superstar' when I walk past, or asking me if I got lost and ended up at the wrong school."

Jack's face crumpled. "That's awful."

"Whatever." Lola smiled, but her face was tight. "I guess not everybody likes a girl who isn't as dull as a pair of old stockings. I mean, I'm not that bad. Am I?" She chuckled like it was a joke, but it didn't seem like one.

"Of course not!" Emmy said.

"You're the best," Jack assured her.

Lola's cheeks went pink and she flicked her hair behind her shoulder. "Anyway, I'm not planning on being here that long. How goes the fight to catch the weaselly little thief?"

"Sam's started going to Latin Society," Jack said. "Hopefully he can keep an eye on both Brynn and Larraby there."

"Don't you think he'll get some idea about the Order if he's at Latin Society all the time?" Lola asked.

"I doubt it," Jack said. "Most people at Latin Society aren't part of the Order. It's just a recruiting ground where they can look at people they think might be a good fit. They only ask a couple of people to join every year, and they're almost always in their last few years at school."

"Sam's been hanging out with us less and less," Emmy said, "so we're going to launch phase two of the plan pretty soon."

"Well, make it quick," Lola grumbled. "I don't want to spend a minute longer at this school than I have to."

Emmy squeezed her hand. "Don't worry, we'll get you back." She sounded more confident than she felt. Phase two was where the plan could all go wrong.

Chapter 11

Phase Two

It was a whole week before they decided they were ready to launch the next phase of their plan. Lola pestered Jack and Emmy about it every day, and with good reason. She'd joined the Erindale soccer team, but her skill on the pitch seemed to make people like her even less.

"I don't get it," she said to Emmy on the phone one day. "Don't they want their team to win?"

Emmy didn't know what to say. She didn't get it, either.

"You guys are doing it tomorrow, right?" Lola said.

"Yeah," Emmy said. "Sam said he's still up for it. I hope people aren't too hard on him."

"He'll be fine," Lola said. "Just get it done, and you'd better make sure your acting skills are brilliant."

"Don't worry. If Sam does what he says he's going to do, I won't have to act too hard."

They said their goodbyes, and Emmy grabbed her soccer gear and ran down to the locker rooms. Madam Boxgrove would be furious if she was late. She was about to put on her cleats when she saw something stuffed inside one of them. It was a jewelry box, one she'd never seen before. Her heart skipped a beat. Was this another message from her dad, like the ones she'd gotten last year?

She opened the box and found a piece of paper folded inside:

I hope you enjoyed your first Medieval Society meeting, as well as your trip to King's Lynn. In case you were wondering, I'm always keeping an eye on you.

Sincerely, Brother Loyola

Emmy's throat went dry. It wasn't from her dad; it was from Jonas. How did he know she'd been in King's Lynn last week? And that she'd joined the Medieval Society?

She tried to ignore how much her fingers were shaking as she tied the laces on her cleats. She shouldn't be surprised that Jonas had somebody watching her, but it still made her skin crawl.

The common room was as busy as ever after dinner the next day. There was no study session that night, so people were huddled around tablets and laptops, watching shows or playing games. Emmy scrolled through her social media feed, but she didn't read a single word of it. She was way too nervous. Jack was sketching next to her, but his hand was shaking a lot more than normal. Finally, they saw what they were waiting for—Brynn came back from dinner and sat down with a couple of friends from Latin Society. Emmy typed out a text: He's here.

Her heart started hammering. How long would it take Sam to come downstairs? She just wanted to get this over with. A few minutes later Sam strolled in and walked right past Jack and Emmy, exactly like he was supposed to. Emmy felt Jack take a deep breath.

"Hey, Sam!" Jack called. "Where were you at supper? We were saving a seat for you."

Sam stuffed an earbud into his ear. "Sorry, I was busy." He kept walking, and Jack stood up.

"Wait," Jack said, "there's a spot at our table. Do you want to work on our physics assignment together?"

"Not really," Sam said.

People at nearby tables were starting to watch them. Sam had walked so far away that Jack practically had to yell so Sam would hear him.

"Oh, well, we don't have to do school work. We could do something else."

Sam whipped around and pulled his earbud out. "Bloody hell, can't you take a hint?" he yelled.

The room got quieter. Anybody within a few feet was watching them now.

"I've tried to be nice," Sam said, "but you're making it impossible!"

Somebody switched off the music. The room was almost totally silent.

"You've been following me around like a lapdog for a

whole month. I just can't take it anymore. I'm sorry your best friend got chucked out of here, but I'm not going to be your new one." Sam stared icily at Jack.

A few boys laughed, and Jack's face crumpled. Emmy didn't know if he was pretending to be upset or not. Even though they'd known what Sam was going to say, it was pretty painful to hear.

Jack looked around the room. His eyes were welling up, which surprised Emmy. He didn't seem to be acting anymore. He ran up the Edmund stairs and Emmy stood up.

"Jack, wait," she called, but he didn't turn back.

"I'll go after him," someone said. It was Cadel, Jack's roommate from the year before. He scowled at Sam as he walked past. "Seriously, what's your problem?"

Sam didn't flinch. He looked straight past Cadel like he hadn't even heard him.

The room started buzzing again. A lot of people were giving Sam dirty looks, but some of the boys were smiling and laughing, which made Emmy's blood boil. Brynn looked at Sam like he was seeing him in a new light and liked what he saw. If Brynn bought Sam's performance, it would make the whole thing worth it.

Emmy wiped imaginary tears off her cheeks and ran to her

room. There were footsteps on the stairs behind her, which meant her part of the performance was only just beginning.

She opened the door to her room and Natalie and Jaya ran in behind her.

"Hey," Natalie said, "oh my gosh, that was horrible. Are you okay?"

Emmy sniffed and started typing on her phone. "Yeah, I'm fine. I'm just trying to find out if Jack's okay." Even though the whole fight was a fake, it didn't feel like it.

"That was so harsh," Jaya said. "I thought Sam was all right, but obviously not."

Emmy felt a pang of guilt. All of Jack's friends would turn on Sam now. The gravity of what Sam was sacrificing started to sink in. Hopefully Brynn would tell him who took the money and they could explain that it had all been a setup, but what if they couldn't? Or what if it took all year?

Emmy checked her phone and bit her lip. "Why won't he answer?" Ignoring his phone was part of Jack's plan— he wanted to seem too upset to talk—but right now all she wanted was to make sure he was really okay.

"I'll check with Cadel," Jaya said as she pulled out her phone.

Emmy sat down on her bed and Natalie put her arm around

her. "Don't worry, Jack's got plenty of friends. He doesn't need that tosser anyway."

Emmy smiled. It was nice to see people rallying around Jack. It reminded her of all the reasons she loved Wellsworth, and why she wanted—needed—to get Lola back here.

Jaya's phone dinged. She tucked her long, black hair behind her shoulder and read. "It's from Cadel. He says Jack seemed upset, but he wanted to be alone for a while."

"Okay," Emmy said. "I guess I'll just wait for him to call then."

"Do you want some company?" Natalie asked.

"Sure." Jack wouldn't call her until Sam turned up in their room, and that probably wouldn't be for a few hours.

Emmy, Natalie, and Jaya chatted about teachers and classes and what movies they were excited to see next. Jaya pretended to be interested when Emmy and Natalie talked about soccer, and Emmy pretended to be interested when Jaya talked about fashion. Natalie showed them some latex makeup she was going to use for Halloween, and they watched a creepy video of someone turning themselves into a werewolf and then peeling off the latex after. Emmy was having such a good time that when her phone finally rang, it made her jump.

"It's Jack," she said, "and it's a video call. Do you mind if—"

"We'll give you guys some space," Natalie said. She and Jaya hurried out the door, and Emmy pressed her phone's green button. Jack's face appeared, and Sam was behind him.

"Hey," she said, "you guys okay?"

"Never better," Sam said with a grin. Jack was smiling too, but he looked tired, like he'd just been through something hard.

"A lot of people are pretty ticked off at you right now."

Sam just laughed. "You don't know the half of it. I think Cadel would have challenged me to a proper duel if he could have found a sword."

"Are you actually enjoying this?" Emmy asked.

"It's the most fun I've had in ages. Fenella Greenborough kept talking loudly about how she was glad she'd figured out who had real class before she asked anybody to the cinema next week." He elbowed Jack. "I guess I shouldn't expect her to ask me out anytime soon."

Emmy felt her ears go pink. It wasn't the worst thing in the world if Sam didn't go to the cinema with Fenella Greenborough.

"I was pretty worried about you for a minute there," Sam said to Jack. "You did a great job of looking like I'd crushed your soul."

Jack laughed. "Yeah, well, it's been awhile since I've been publicly humiliated."

Emmy winced. It must have brought up some pretty tough memories of how Brynn used to treat Jack.

"You sure you're okay?" she asked.

He nodded, and even though he still looked tired, his smile seemed genuine. "I've spent the last two hours getting messages from people telling me how great I am. I've never been this popular in my life!"

Everybody laughed.

"Unfortunately, half of Edmund and Audrey Houses aren't speaking to Sam anymore," Jack said.

Sam shrugged. "It was totally worth it. Jamie and Rhys came and sat with me, and they're two of Brynn's best friends. Hopefully I'll get in good with him soon enough. If I can get him to blab, this'll all be over."

Emmy nodded. He'd better be right.

Over the next few weeks, Sam started spending more and more time with Brynn. They walked to class together, hung out in the common room together, and went to Latin Society together. He was keeping an eye on Larraby too, but so far he hadn't noticed anything unusual. Emmy knew it would take time for Sam to really earn Brynn's trust, but she wished they could speed up the process. She also wondered if she should warn him about the Order now that he was spending so much time at Latin Society, but she always decided not to. It was too risky to let someone else in on that secret.

Emmy was on the way to Medieval Society when she felt her phone buzzing in her bag. She frowned. Everybody had societies, so her friends never called right after school, and her mom never called until after dinner. She fished around for her phone and was about to turn it off when she saw it was Lola calling.

Emmy pressed send. "Hey, what's up?" She could hear sniffling on the other end of the phone.

"Got in a fight," Lola said.

Emmy straightened up. "Seriously? Are you okay?"

"Um, yeah. My face is hurting pretty bad, and my hand is killing me from trying to hit them back."

"*Them?!* There was more than one of them?"

"Yeah, just two. I managed to stay off the ground, though, otherwise it would have been a lot worse."

Emmy thought of Lola being cornered, two to one, how scared she must have been, and how she didn't have anyone there to stick up for her. She started to cry. "Do you need a doctor? Does your dad know?"

"Yeah, he's here. He cleaned me up already. I haven't told mum yet, though. She's going to flip."

Emmy kept crying.

"Don't do that, Em." Lola's voice quivered. "I won't be able to stand it."

"I just… You…" Emmy swallowed and wiped her eyes. "You could have been hurt really badly. What if they attack you again?"

"I don't think they will." She laughed bitterly. "They didn't look so good, either. Hopefully that'll be enough for them not to try again. But Dad's going to pick me up from school from now on just in case. That way I won't have to walk home by myself."

"Do you want me to see if I can come for the weekend again?"

Lola made a noise that sounded like a cross between a sigh and a sob. "That'd be great."

Madam Boyd took Emmy to Lola's as soon as school let out on Friday. Jack's art teacher had arranged for him to take a livestreamed painting workshop that weekend, and even though he was excited about it, he was pretty gutted about staying behind. He started getting fidgety if he didn't hear from Lola every few hours, and Emmy didn't blame him. She was worried, too.

Lucy hadn't been happy when Emmy had texted her about going to King's Lynn, but Emmy didn't care. Nothing was going to keep her away from Lola right now.

Madam Boyd had been going back and forth to King's Lynn all week and was looking a lot more tired than usual. Lola was still at soccer practice when they got to King's Lynn, so Madam Boyd drove straight to Erindale.

"I have a meeting with the headmaster," Madam Boyd said swiftly. "And he'd better have a plan for how to deal with all this."

Emmy smothered a smile. She didn't envy that headmaster having to face Madam Boyd in this mood.

Emmy walked past a teacher stuffing papers into his satchel and then went to the playing fields at the back of the school. She sat on a bench and watched the scrimmage. Even from this distance the bruises on Lola's face stood out. They didn't seem to affect her play, though. She was barking out signals and faking out defenders like they were standing still. A man sat down next to her and watched the scrimmage, too. *Probably a parent*, she thought.

"She's a good player, isn't she, young miss?"

Emmy froze. She didn't look up. She didn't have to. There was only one person who called her that.

Her hands started to shake. Should she run? Should she scream? Jonas wouldn't try to hurt her in broad daylight with all these people around...would he?

"Have you given any more thought to my proposal?" he asked.

Emmy lifted her chin. She could at least look confident even if she didn't feel it. "I don't know where my dad is, Jonas. I couldn't tell you even if I wanted to."

She saw him nod out of the corner of her eye. "I feel like you haven't been trying that hard."

"I haven't seen him in ten years. What do you expect me to do?"

"But you've heard from him."

Emmy's stomach dropped. How did he know she'd heard from her dad?

Jonas kept watching the soccer scrimmage, as if it were totally normal for him to be sitting on that bench. "You are a curious young lady. I suppose there's nothing wrong with that. You know what makes me curious? How you got those medallions in the first place."

Now it was Emmy's turn to be silent. She wasn't about to give him any information he didn't already have.

"I see you're not feeling up to sharing today," Jonas said. "It would be so much easier if I could ask Tom my questions instead."

"I can't help you. I told you, I don't know where he is."

Jonas looked back at the field. "Such a shame about what happened this week. I hope she wasn't too banged up."

A slimy feeling crept up Emmy's throat. How could Jonas possibly know about Lola's fight? Unless...

"The Order's behind her having a hard time here, isn't it," she said. "Somebody from the Order told those girls to jump her."

"Money talks, love, even to teenagers."

"Well, you'll have a hard time getting them to do it again," Emmy said. "Lola gave as good as she got."

Jonas laughed quietly. "You don't think that'll be the end of it, do you?"

Emmy's heart thudded in her chest.

"This is only the beginning for Miss Boyd. She could switch schools, she could move away, but we'd always find her. And like I said, money will always talk. Who knows what might happen to her next?"

He may as well have put his hand around Emmy's throat. She couldn't breathe. She couldn't think. The Order was coming after Lola, and they weren't going to stop until they got what they wanted.

"If you value your friend's life, I'd suggest you try a little harder to find your dear old dad."

Then Jonas stood up and walked away.

Chapter 12

Back and Forth

E mmy didn't say a word to Lola about what Jonas had said on the bench. What was the point? It would just scare her, and there was nothing they could do about it. The only person who could keep the Order away from Lola was Emmy, but that would mean betraying her father.

The one thing she wished they could talk about was how Jonas knew she'd be in King's Lynn. It didn't make sense for him to be watching Lola twenty-four-seven. He had to have known that Emmy would be at her school. But how?

It was a quiet trip back to school with Madam Boyd on Sunday night. Soccer matches were starting soon, which meant Emmy wouldn't be able to go to King's Lynn on the weekends. The separation between her and Lola was starting to feel more real, like it was the norm. Emmy didn't like that feeling.

Madam Boyd cleared her throat. "I was just wondering, and of course you don't have to tell me if you don't think it's appropriate, but have you heard from your father lately?"

Emmy fiddled with her seat belt. Her dad was the last person she wanted to talk about.

"I only hear from him through you or Barlowe," Emmy said. "Why? Have you heard from him?"

"Neither of us has heard from him since term started." Madam Boyd glanced at Emmy. "But that's not unusual. I'm sure you don't need to worry."

"I wasn't." If the Order had gotten to her dad, Jonas wouldn't be threatening Emmy's friends. Her dad was fine. For now.

She rubbed her hand on the armrest. There was a question she'd never asked Madam Boyd, but it had been on her mind for a while. "Did my dad ever ask you about what happened with the safe-deposit box?"

"No," Boyd said, "I assumed it was a personal matter."

"So, he doesn't know I opened a second one?"

"Not that I'm aware of." Boyd glanced at her. "Should I have told him?"

"I was just following his instructions," Emmy lied. She'd better change the subject. "How does he communicate with you?"

Madam Boyd tapped her fingers on the steering wheel. "I think it's best for you to know as little about that as possible."

"Why?"

"Because contact with your father would put you in danger."

"So why is Dad okay with putting other people in danger? He has no problem talking to you and Barlowe. Why can't he talk to me for once?"

"You're his child," Boyd said gently. "Nothing's more important to him than you are."

Emmy wasn't so sure about that. "Do you know why he sent me to that bank?"

"Of course not. Like I said, I assumed it was personal."

"Well, it wasn't. It was about the Order. It's always about the Order."

Boyd didn't say anything, and Emmy was glad. She was tired of talking about the Order. She was tired of thinking about them and trying to outsmart them. She just wanted her friends to be safe.

She leaned her head against the car window and watched the rain dribble down the glass. Why had her dad ever gotten her involved in all this in the first place? If it hadn't been for that very first letter he'd sent her, she never would have found the medallions. Brynn never would have figured out she had a connection to the Order, and Jonas never would have come after her. She and Jack and Lola would be sitting in the common room right now playing one of Lola's card games. Instead, she was trying to figure out how to keep her best friend alive.

When she got back to the common room, she found Jack sitting with Cadel and Natalie. He jumped up when he saw her.

"Hey, how is she?" His voice was shaky. "Is she okay?"

Emmy didn't even know how to answer that. "She's not too excited to go back to school tomorrow, but she says she's feeling okay. Weren't you texting her all weekend?"

"Yeah, but you actually *saw* her. That's different. She's a way better liar when she's using her phone."

"Are those girls going to get in trouble?" Natalie asked.

"She doesn't know. Madam Boyd reamed out their school's headmaster on Friday, and he swears he's going to do something, but..." Emmy shrugged. The Order might find a way to get them out of trouble. The Order always got what it wanted.

"How was your workshop?" Emmy asked.

Jack's eyes lit up. "Amazing. It was all about painting faces and capturing a feeling. Master Kenneth says there's another one next month."

Emmy smiled. Jack's whole demeanor changed when he talked about art, like someone flicked on a hidden light inside him. Emmy looked around the room. Sam was sitting nearby, along with Brynn and another guy from Latin Society. Sam's hair wasn't as messy as usual, and it looked like he was wearing a new polo shirt. Emmy had thought watching him cozy up to Brynn might make him less attractive, but she was dead wrong. He was sacrificing a lot for Lola, even though he barely knew her. She imagined being with Sam, Lola, and Jack, sitting around the fire, just being normal friends. And maybe being more than friends with Sam.

Sam said something and the whole table laughed while Brynn clapped him on the shoulder. If Sam was trying to make it seem like Brynn was influencing him, it seemed to be working. Maybe Sam was getting somewhere. If only she could ask Jack what was happening, but they couldn't talk about it with Brynn three feet away, and it would look pretty suspicious if the two of them went outside to talk in the pouring rain. They'd have to wait until tomorrow, and hopefully Lola would still be okay by then.

Emmy was so worried about Lola that she could barely concentrate in her classes the next day. She went blank during a math quiz and didn't even fill out half the answers. Lucy was going to flip when she found out Emmy had failed a test.

Emmy texted Lola as soon as she started walking back to Audrey House after her last class.

How was school today?

Delightfully dull, Lola responded.

No trouble with anybody today?

Nothing but dirty looks.

Emmy closed her eyes and breathed out. Hopefully Jonas would give her time before he made his next move.

Try to stay out of people's way, okay?

It was a few moments before Lola responded.

I'll stay out of their way if they stay out of mine.

Emmy rubbed her forehead. Maybe Lola should know that she was dealing with more than just a couple of disgruntled girls. Then again, that would probably just make her madder, and the last thing they needed was Lola losing her temper.

Somebody requested for my locker to be moved. It's right next to the office now. Should be a lot safer.

Do you know who it was?

No idea. I thought someone in the office had done it themselves, but when I asked about it, they said they thought I'd put in the request myself.

Weird. I guess someone around there is looking out for you.

Lola sent an eye roll emoji.

Don't get sappy. It was probably Mum, but she doesn't want me to think she's interfering.

Maybe.

Emmy didn't really think so, though. Who would want to help Lola anonymously? And why?

Emmy walked into the forest, but instead of turning toward Audrey House, she took the path that went deeper into the woods. She scampered over the roots and fallen pine branches until the ground got softer and the trees got thinner. Finally, the forest disappeared, replaced by an almost endless mud flat with towering cliffs on either side.

Jack and Sam were waiting for her.

"You guys didn't come out here together, did you?" she asked.

Sam shook his head. "I skived off humanities, so I've been out here an hour already."

"You skipped class? Uh, that doesn't go over very well at Wellsworth," Emmy said.

Sam shrugged. "All they do is tell your head of house, and it's not like Larraby's going to care. He's a bit of an odd bloke, Larraby. He doesn't talk much about Latin at Latin Society."

Emmy cleared her throat. "What does he talk about?" She'd gone to Latin Society all of last year, but Larraby had usually steered clear of her.

"Hang on," Jack said. "I'm going to call Lola so she can hear this." He clicked her picture on his phone and pressed the button for a video call. Soon her picture was replaced by the living version.

"Bloody hell," she said, "if I'd known it was all three of you, I would have brushed my hair."

"No, you wouldn't," Jack said.

"Fair enough. So, what's up?"

"Sam's just giving us a bit of an update," Emmy said.

"On Brynn?" Lola asked eagerly.

"On Larraby." Jack looked at Sam. "So, what has he been talking about?"

"He tells a lot of stories and loads of bad jokes. It's funny, though. There are about five or six guys who always hang around after Latin Society's done. Brynn's one of them, and he says they like to stay and chat with Larraby for a while."

Jack shuffled his feet and glanced at Emmy. Was this when the Order was having their meetings now? Five or six people didn't seem like very many, but maybe the group at school was smaller than they'd thought, or maybe other people joined them from a secret passage.

"Has Brynn ever asked you to stay?" Jack asked.

"Nah." Sam laughed. "He probably knows that two hours at Latin Society is plenty of time with Larraby for me!"

Emmy laughed and hoped it didn't sound too awkward.

"How's Oliver doing?" Jack asked.

"Seems fine. Larraby's not leaving him out or anything. Well, not that he could anyway, not with Vincent around."

Jack just about dropped the phone. "Vincent? Like, my brother?"

"Yeah." Sam stared at him. "Didn't you know he comes to Latin Society all the time?"

"Uh, no, I definitely didn't."

"He's there almost every week. He's a bloody genius when it comes to Latin, so he volunteers with us. Says it's good for his résumé."

Emmy and Jack looked at each other. Vincent's role in the Order must have expanded now that Jonas wasn't here. He might even be passing messages between Jonas and Larraby.

"What's going on with Brynn?" Lola asked.

"I think I'm pretty much in with him," Sam said. "He's always asking me to sit with him at lunch and at Latin Society, and we hang out a lot in the evenings."

Lola's eyes went wide. "Already? That's brilliant! It's only been a couple of weeks."

Emmy frowned. Now that she thought about it, it was strange that their friendship had happened so fast. Brynn was usually so guarded.

"Yeah, well, he likes people who are total prats," Sam said. His voice sounded heavier than usual, like something was weighing him down.

"Has he talked about me yet?" Lola asked.

"Yep."

Jack almost dropped the phone. "You didn't tell me that!"

"It was at lunch today," Sam said. "Somebody said something about Lola never being able to get away with stealing all that money. Then he smiled and said, 'My cousin may be weird, but she's not smart enough to be a thief.'"

"Hey!" Lola said. "Is he calling me stupid? 'Cause I'm plenty smart enough to pull off a heist like that."

Emmy rolled her eyes. "Seriously, Lola, is that what you're going to fixate on right now?"

"I'm just saying, I'm not—"

"Can we please focus on the fact that Brynn just admitted that he knows you didn't take that money?" Jack said.

Lola slumped against her bedroom wall. "Whatever."

"What else did he say?" Jack asked.

"I looked at him and said, 'Are you telling me she didn't actually take it?' And he just winked and said, 'I wouldn't know anything about that, mate.'"

"He called you 'mate'?" Jack said. "He really is slumming with you if he's talking like you now."

"I guess." Sam kicked at the dirt.

"Is everything okay?" Emmy asked.

"Yeah, no, it's fine, I just… You guys are *sure* it was him, right?"

"Definitely," Emmy said.

"Why?"

Nobody said anything at first. They couldn't explain the whole reason why.

"He's got an axe to grind," Jack said, "and you heard what

he said. 'I wouldn't know anything about that, mate'? That wink was practically admitting that he did it."

Sam kept twisting his toe in the mud. He definitely didn't seem as sure as everyone else.

"Do you want to stop doing this?" Emmy asked softly.

"Wait, what?" Lola said. "I'm kind of dying over here."

"But what if Brynn doesn't have anything to do with that?" Sam said. "I looked at the footage again, and I'm sure Brynn wasn't in the office at all that night."

"He could have had an accomplice," Jack said.

"Okay, but if that's true, it could have been somebody else entirely then, right?"

Emmy didn't know what to say. It was killing her to keep Sam in the dark. But she couldn't keep her dad's warning out of her head. Trust no one.

"I've known Brynn a long time," Jack said. "I know it's him."

"There's nothing you guys aren't telling me, is there?"

"What do you mean?" Jack asked way too quickly.

"I don't know," Sam said. "Sometimes I just get the impression that there's something I don't know."

Lola laughed. "You think those two could keep a secret? Jack lied to a teacher once about why he hadn't done his homework and he practically wet his pants."

Sam laughed. "Yeah, I bet." He looked down at the ground. "Are you *sure* there isn't anything you're not telling me?"

Emmy's head hurt. She wanted to tell Sam the truth so much, but it wasn't safe. Not for him, and not for her.

"Really, there's nothing," Jack said a bit too forcefully.

Sam looked at each of them. Emmy couldn't tell whether he believed them, and it made her heart ache.

"Well, I'd better go," Sam said. "I've got to figure out what I'm going to tell people about where I've been all afternoon. See ya."

They all said goodbye and Sam disappeared into the trees.

"Do you think he bought it?" Emmy asked.

"You're fine," Lola said.

"Do we really have to keep the Order a secret from him?" Jack asked. "I mean, he's really sticking his neck out for us. I feel bad not telling him the whole truth."

"I know," Emmy said, "but we can't. If we told him about the Order, he could let something slip to Brynn by accident."

"Besides," Lola said, "he might not be able to act so easily around Brynn if he knew he was more than just a run-of-the-mill prat."

"I guess," Jack said. "I just don't want it to be like we're just using him, you know?"

Emmy bit her lip. Jack had a point.

"He knew what he was getting into," Lola said. "He wants to help because he wants Brynn to get what's coming to him."

"I guess," Jack said.

"Look," Lola said, "I don't care what you have to do to get me out of this place. If you have to send Sam and Brynn on a Caribbean cruise, just do it. And preferably before Erindale plays Wellsworth at football, 'cause I don't know if I can take that."

Emmy tucked her hair behind her ear. If Jonas made good on his threats, Lola would have a lot more than soccer to worry about.

Chapter 13

Thirteen Candles

Another week went by, and Sam still hadn't gotten any information out of Brynn. He didn't seem to be hanging around Brynn as much, which was making all of them nervous. He often didn't get back to their room until Jack was asleep, so Jack couldn't check in to make sure everything was okay. Lola was having almost daily problems at school, and Emmy was starting to panic. Even if they did clear Lola's name, would the Order leave her alone? She'd probably be safer at Wellsworth where she had her friends around her all the time, but what if the Order found another way to get her kicked out? Jonas said he wouldn't stop until Emmy gave up her dad. Even if Sam got the info they needed, it might not be enough.

One night, Jack and Emmy were playing a half-hearted game of Slap It when Natalie came into the common room. Jaya was holding her by the elbow, and she had a bandage around two of her fingers.

"What happened?" Emmy asked.

"She fell down the stairs," Jaya said.

Emmy's jaw dropped. "What?"

"Are you okay?" Jack asked.

"I sprained a couple fingers, and I hit my head." She gingerly put her fingers on a purple welt on her forehead. "It doesn't seem too bad, but the nurse said I shouldn't play football for at least a week just in case. Mostly I'm just black and blue."

Emmy stood up. "Let's get you upstairs." She and Jaya stood on either side of Natalie as she went up all four flights.

"Seriously, I'm fine," Natalie said as she slowly sat down on her bed.

"How did it happen?" Emmy asked.

"It all happened so fast, I don't really remember it." Natalie pushed herself back with her good hand and leaned against her pillows. "It's weird, though. I didn't think anybody else was on the stairs, but I swear I remember somebody bumping into me from behind."

Emmy's mouth went dry. "Do you think somebody might have pushed you? Like, on purpose?"

"Nah," Natalie said, "why would somebody do that? Either it was an accident, or I imagined it."

Emmy didn't say anything. The Order didn't have anything against Natalie, but what was it Barlowe had said? Sometimes going after a loved one is more effective. She closed her eyes. The thought of the Order going after her roommate was terrifying. Wasn't anybody around her safe?

Emmy helped Natalie get settled and then grabbed her design and technology textbook. She couldn't afford to keep falling behind. She flicked on her reading lamp and was about to nestle into her covers when she saw something lying on her pillow. It was an envelope with her name on it.

Her fingers shook while she opened it. Whatever was inside couldn't be good. She pulled out a piece of paper and began to read:

Sorry you're struggling in mathematics.
Your dad wasn't any good at it, either.

It wasn't signed. It didn't have to be. Jonas was the only one who'd write her something like that.

Emmy tossed her textbook on the floor and curled up under her covers. How did Jonas know so much? Knowing she had joined the Medieval Society was one thing—anybody could have seen her going—but knowing that she'd failed a math quiz? And how did he always know when she was in King's Lynn? If he was trying to make her think he had spies everywhere, it was working.

One week later, Emmy's alarm seemed to ring extra early. She reached to push the off button on her cell and realized it wasn't an alarm, it was a phone call.

"Hello?" she said groggily.

"Happy birthday, darling!"

Emmy smiled. "Thanks, Mom."

"What are you going to buy with the money I sent you?"

"I'm not sure. I should get to go into King's Lynn in a couple of weeks, and I can go shopping with Lola then."

There was a long pause. "You're still seeing Lola? I thought she was kicked out."

"Yeah, she lives in King's Lynn, so I can still see her on the weekends sometimes."

"Darling, I'm not sure that spending time with a troublemaker is such a good idea."

Emmy frowned. "Lola's not a troublemaker. Somebody framed her for something she didn't do."

"That's not what I heard."

"What do you mean?"

"Lucy knows some Wellsworth parents, and they have very serious concerns about this girl."

Some Wellsworth parents. Those must be the people who didn't want them in that club. People who were probably part of the Order.

"Lucy told me that Lola has been getting into trouble since her very first year," her mom went on. "Apparently she's gotten into fights, and I think she even punched her cousin."

"Her cousin's a jerk," Emmy said. She didn't mention that *she* had once punched Lola's cousin, too.

"That's not the point." Her mom sighed. "I don't want to tell you that you can't hang out with this girl anymore, but—"

"No way."

"Emmeline—"

"No!" Emmy didn't care what people had told Lucy. There was no way she was going to let Lola go.

Her mom didn't say anything right away. "Like I said, I don't want to have to tell you that you can't see her. I just want you to be on your guard. Don't let her influence your choices."

Emmy swiped a tear off her cheek. How was she supposed to defend Lola to her own mother? "Anything else?"

"Do you have any plans for your birthday?" her mom asked quietly.

"Nope." Her voice had a distinct edge to it now.

"All right. I love you, Emmy."

Emmy wiped more tears away. "Bye."

"Goodbye, darling. Happy birthday." The phone went dead.

Emmy was so mad she didn't know how to stop crying. She didn't know what was more frustrating: the fact that her mom wanted her to stop being Lola's friend, or the fact that she was taking Lucy's word over hers.

The blankets on the bed across the room rustled, and Natalie emerged from the covers. The bruise on her forehead was almost gone, and she was moving much more easily now. "Was that your mum?"

Emmy nodded.

Natalie got out of her bed and sat down on Emmy's. "She thinks Lola's a troublemaker, huh?"

"Her cousin told her all kinds of stuff about Lola, and now she doesn't want me to hang out with her anymore. It's not like I can abandon her right now."

Natalie put her arm around Emmy's shoulder. "Lola's a big girl, she can take care of herself."

Emmy couldn't tell Natalie why that wasn't true this time. Sure, Lola could handle a bully. But she couldn't handle an entire secret society on her own.

Emmy got a lot of birthday wishes that day. Cadel and Jack sang a terribly off-key version of "Happy Birthday," and Jaya wrapped her in a beautiful, sage-green scarf because she said birthdays should be "fancy." It seemed like people were making an extra effort because they knew Emmy would be sad that her best friend wasn't there to celebrate with her. At first all the extra attention was fun, but by the time she made her way to humanities, she felt worse instead of better.

All these wishes reminded her that she was surrounded by

people who cared, and Lola had no one, at least not until she got home to her dad at the end of the day.

She was just about at the classroom door when she saw Sam coming down the hall. Her heart skipped a beat. They hadn't gotten a chance to talk much lately.

"Hey," she said.

"Hey."

"Um, how's it going?" she asked.

"Good."

Emmy swallowed. She knew he wasn't supposed to be friendly with her, not when he was still trying to get close to Brynn, but... *Was* he still trying to get close to Brynn? She stared into his big brown eyes, and suddenly she needed to know. She needed to know if he was still pretending to be distant, or if something had happened to make it real. Maybe they could find a place to talk later, without other people around. Just the two of them.

Emmy twisted her fingers together. People were jostling past them to get to humanities. She kept smiling and nodding her head, like this wasn't awkward at all, which made it even *more* awkward. She tried to take a deep breath, but her lungs seemed to have shrunk. She was just asking a friend to chat. That was a totally normal, everyday thing to do. It's not like she was asking him to go out with her. That would be unheard of. Wouldn't it?

She looked around to make sure nobody was listening. "So, I was wondering—"

"There's nothing new going on with Brynn," he said quickly. "Or with Larraby."

Emmy blinked.

"If that's what you were asking," Sam said.

"Um, it wasn't."

"Oh."

They both looked at the floor. Now what? If she asked him to talk alone, he'd think it was all about Brynn. He probably thought that was all she cared about. She needed to say something that would convince him that she genuinely liked him, but without telling him that she *liked* him.

She smiled and nodded some more.

Say something.

Something brilliant and funny and delightful, something that would make him laugh instead of staring at his shoes.

Say something!

But what if it was the wrong something? What if was something even worse than smiling and nodding your head at someone for a full minute?

"So, what were you going to ask?" Sam finally said.

"I, um, I just…" It was like someone had erased a blackboard inside her head. Every word she'd ever learned was gone. All she could think of was how badly she wanted to melt into the floor. "I guess I forgot," she mumbled.

"Oh. Okay."

Part of her thought he looked disappointed. At least, she wished he looked disappointed.

He walked into class and Emmy leaned her back against the wall. This birthday couldn't get much worse. She waited until the last moment to slip into class so she wouldn't have to talk to anybody else.

"Afternoon, everyone," Barlowe said from the platform at the bottom of the round classroom. "I hope by now you are all comfortable with the events surrounding the first English Civil War. When we last left King Charles the First, his army had been wiped out and he was lounging in a rather comfortable imprisonment in a castle on the Isle of Wight. He pretended to start negotiating with the Parliamentary army that had defeated him, and most Parliamentarians thought they would come to an agreement where Parliament and the Monarchy would govern together. Unfortunately, like many British monarchs before him, he preferred intrigue to negotiation. He betrayed them. He secretly engaged the Scots in a plot to attack the Parliamentary army."

Natalie raised her hand. "Why would Scotland do that? I thought they didn't like the King."

"He made promises that would have given Scotland much more freedom and independence. However, chances are the King eventually would have betrayed Scotland, too. He had already shown that he would betray allies on a whim, so why would Scotland be any different?"

"But why would other people trust him after that?" Natalie asked.

Barlowe smiled. "You have to understand that betrayals have been part of political life since the dawn of politics itself. Brutus betrayed Caesar during the golden age of Rome, Henry the Second betrayed Thomas Becket in the twelfth century, and it goes on and on. Sometimes greed and power become stronger than friendship. In that case, betrayal becomes almost inevitable."

Emmy looked at her fingernails. Her dad had said that he and Jonas were best friends, but they still betrayed each other. Was it just Jonas's need for power that destroyed their friendship? Or was her father to blame, too?

Even with all the stuff happening with Sam, she couldn't

get her dad out of her head. If she found out where he was, she could tell Jonas and get Lola back. She wasn't even sure if that would be a betrayal; it's not like she was friends with her dad. Or had any kind of relationship with him, really. And if she did nothing, it was like she was betraying her best friend. She was the only person who could save Lola. If she didn't do it, it was like she was handing *Lola* over to the Order. That felt a lot more like a betrayal than handing over her dad. And what if the Order had hurt Natalie, too? She had to stop this.

But how? She didn't know where her dad was, so there was nothing to tell Jonas anyway. But if she was able to find out, at least then she'd have the choice of whether to save Lola, or whether to save her dad.

After class, Emmy waited beside Barlowe's desk until everyone else had gone.

"What can I help you with, Miss Willick?"

"I wanted to talk to you about that extracurricular project we were discussing a few weeks ago."

Barlowe raised an eyebrow. "Of course. Why don't we go for a walk?"

The wind whipped Emmy's hair across her face as they walked toward a wide-open clearing in the middle of the grounds. Anyone would be able to see them, but it would be nearly impossible to get close enough to eavesdrop.

"How is Miss Boyd doing at her new school?"

Emmy didn't answer right away. If Barlowe knew the Order was giving Lola trouble, he'd be suspicious of why Emmy wanted to talk about her dad.

"She's doing okay," Emmy said.

"I'm glad to hear it."

They reached the clearing, and Barlowe took a quick look around. "All right Emmy, what's going on? Is anybody giving you any trouble? You haven't heard from Jonas or any other Order member, have you?"

Emmy paused. Part of her wanted to tell Barlowe everything. At least there'd be an adult to help. But what could he do? If he could have stopped the Order, he would have done it a long time ago.

"It's about my dad," she said.

He clasped his hands behind his back. "What about him?"

"You're in touch with him, right?"

He nodded slowly.

"I know you don't know exactly where he is, but… I was just wondering… See, it's my birthday. I'm thirteen today."

"Happy birthday," he said quietly.

"Yeah, thanks. In America it's kind of a big deal when you turn thirteen, and I was kind of hoping maybe I could like, talk to him or something." She hung her head. "So, I wouldn't have another birthday without him." She didn't look up. She felt kind of bad for intentionally tugging at Barlowe's heart strings, but it was the only thing she could think of.

Barlowe let out a heavy sigh. "I'm sorry Emmy, but your father's been very clear. No direct contact with you. It's too dangerous."

She didn't look up. Real emotion was sparking in her now. "Why does he get to decide that?"

"Emmy, you've got to understand, the Order of Black Hollow Lane is a massive criminal organization."

"I've heard there are only like six people going to their meetings right now," Emmy said. "That doesn't seem like a massive organization."

Barlowe looked stunned. "How do you—"

"I'm not telling you how I know." If Barlowe wasn't going to give up information, she wasn't, either.

Barlowe rubbed his forehead and then suddenly stopped, as if he remembered that they were having a conversation that should look casual to anyone who walked past. He rolled his shoulders back and managed a thin smile.

"Emmy, think about it. Yes, they only recruit a handful of people from Wellsworth each year, but people don't leave the Order once they leave school. Their membership is only just beginning. So, let's say they recruit five teenagers a year. The average teenager is going to live at least another fifty years, so let's multiply those five by fifty. They also recruit a number of people from the general public, so even if there are only twenty new members every year... Well, I'll let you do the math."

Emmy's mouth felt dry. There might be thousands of Order members out there.

"Remember that they're not just taking anybody. They recruit in the intelligence service, in policing, in the highest levels of government. So, all those members you're imagining right now are some of the most highly trained, most influential people in Britain. Those are the people your father is on the run from. He knows better than anyone how dangerous they are."

Anger flared inside her and she didn't bother to hide it. "If he knows how dangerous they are, then why did he get me involved in all this in the first place? When he sent me that first letter, he made sure I'd find the box of medallions. And then he kept sending me stuff that got me more and more involved. And in case neither of you have noticed, not having direct contact with him hasn't exactly kept me safe."

"Is somebody threatening you again?" Barlowe asked. "If someone's coming after you, I need to know."

"Nobody's coming after me," Emmy said truthfully. She wasn't the Order's target right now. "I'm just sick of my dad knowing so much about my life and me knowing nothing about his." She folded her arms across her chest. "I want to know where he is."

Barlowe shook is head. "Out of the question."

"Says who?"

"Says your father, Madam Boyd, and myself. We've all agreed to help keep you safe."

"You haven't actually seen him in what, like fifteen years?"

"About that."

"He lied to Madam Boyd about dying in a car crash in England, and he lied to me and my mother about why he disappeared. What makes you so sure you can trust him?"

"I know what his motives are," Barlowe said. "He loves his family so much that he's willing to give up seeing them so he can save their lives. He wants to see the Order taken down. These are all pretty noble motivations, don't you think?"

"If they're real," she said. "Did you know he asked me if I had saved any of the medallions when I threw that box in the ocean?"

"Of course he asked you," Barlowe said. "I believe I asked you, too."

"Right, but he's so obsessed with them that he asked me to put anything I saved into his safe-deposit box in London."

"*Did* you save any of them?" Barlowe raised his eyebrows. "Because even a small number would be useful."

Emmy shook her head and laughed bitterly. "You're just as bad as he is. It's always about the medallions, always about the Order. You guys don't care about me, you only care about how you can use me, just like Jonas does."

Barlowe looked as if she had slapped him. "Your father isn't using you, and neither am I."

"Then prove it. Tell me how I can find my dad, and maybe I'll finally believe you two care about me."

Barlowe closed his eyes, then shook his head. "No. I won't put you in any more danger than you've already been in."

Emmy wanted to scream. She wasn't a little girl anymore. She'd dealt with more danger than most adults had, and yet Barlowe and her dad were convinced she couldn't handle talking to her dad on the phone. Or maybe her dad just didn't *want* to talk to her on the phone. Maybe he didn't even want any contact with her. He just wanted the medallions back.

"You know, I'm glad I threw all those medallions into the sea. I wouldn't have wanted Thomas Allyn to get them either." She spun on her heel and stormed back to Audrey House. This was definitely her worst birthday ever.

Chapter 14

Wellsworth vs. Erindale

The weather was wet and miserable on Saturday. Not stormy, just heavy from three days of constant dribbling that soaked the ground, the air, and the people. Stormy weather would have been better. Storms meant soccer matches were canceled. But it didn't matter how mucky the Wellsworth pitch was, they were still playing Erindale.

Emmy ran in one spot, lifting her knees high to keep out the chill. It helped with the nerves. She didn't know what it would be like to be on opposite sides with Lola. When Erindale took the pitch, a lot of people in the stands yelled at Lola and waved. She didn't wave back. A couple of Erindale girls shook their heads and gave Lola dirty looks. Emmy saw one of them mouth the word *traitor*.

The players took their positions and the whistle blew. Emmy tried not to think about Lola on the other end of the pitch. She had her hands full with the Erindale defenders. They weren't the most skilled team she'd ever played, but they were scrappy, and they weren't afraid to throw a few elbows. Natalie was fully healed and was defending Lola well. She was used to Lola's game from all the scrimmages they'd played over the years. Lola's teammates were getting frustrated with her.

"You're not even trying!" one of them yelled after Lola missed a shot.

"I'm only one person," Lola snapped. "If you want us to score a goal, get your butt up the pitch faster."

Things got worse in the second half. Natalie blocked Lola in the penalty area and kicked the ball down the field. A Wellsworth midfielder took control and Emmy got ready to strike.

"How come your girl Loopy plays so well against every team but yours?" one of the defenders said as she tried to stay between Emmy and the ball. Emmy's insides boiled, but she didn't say anything. This girl just wanted to rile her up.

The midfielder was getting closer, but Emmy still couldn't get out from behind her defender.

"She sure gets bothered easily and is bloody full of herself, too," the girl said. "Bet you were glad to be shod of her. I know we would be."

The midfielder kicked the ball high toward the goal. Emmy jumped for it, but her timing was off. The defender headed the ball back down the field and laughed. "I guess you get bothered pretty easily, too."

Emmy ran to the midfield line just to be rid of the girl. The ball was well inside the Wellsworth zone now. One of the Erindale midfielders passed the ball to Lola, who passed it to one of the forwards. Lola kept pace with her, and she passed it back.

Come on, Lola, come on. At this point Emmy barely cared who won. She just wanted her friend to be okay.

Lola edged into the penalty area. Suddenly she ran straight at Natalie. Natalie stood her ground, but Emmy could tell that she wasn't ready for whatever Lola was about to do.

"Ram right into her!" the Erindale forward yelled.

Suddenly Lola twisted and pulled the ball around Natalie's right. Natalie stuck out her foot and tugged at the ball, but it just went closer to Lola. Lola's cleat bounced off the top and she went flying, landing face-first in the soggy grass. She got up right away, wiping mud and grass off her face with her jersey. Natalie kicked the ball off the pitch, and Lola looked at the official with her hands in the air.

"Play on," the official said.

"Are you completely barmy?" Lola yelled. "She tripped me! It's a penalty shot."

"I didn't," Natalie protested. "I was going for the ball."

"Shut it, Nat, you've been fouling me all day."

Natalie looked dumbfounded. She'd been tough, but Emmy hadn't seen a single foul.

The official grabbed the ball and put it on the sideline. "Erindale ball."

An Erindale forward picked up the ball, but Lola wasn't done with the referee yet. "Are you bloody blind? I got a face full of grass here, and you're not going to do anything about it?"

The referee turned her back on Lola and kept saying "Play on, play on," but Lola wouldn't leave her alone. She was always passionate on the pitch, but Emmy had never seen her like this, especially over such a minor call. Something inside her had snapped. Her language got considerably more colorful, and the referee was having a harder time ignoring her.

Other Erindale girls started laughing. It was like they didn't even care if she got sent off. Natalie put her arm in front Lola's shoulders and tried to pull her back, but Lola shoved her away.

Finally, the ref had enough. She put her hand into her top pocket.

Please just a yellow card, please just a yellow card.

The official pulled out a card. It was red.

Lola's eyes practically bugged out of her head. She kept protesting, but the ref just shook her head and pointed to the sidelines. Lola was being sent off.

A few Erindale players clapped and cheered, and Emmy's eyes filled with hot tears. No one deserved to be treated the way those girls treated Lola. The Wellsworth crowd seemed to think so too, because they started to boo. The Erindale girls just cheered louder.

Finally, Lola stomped off the field. She kept her head up all the way to the locker room. She banged her head on the door and her shoulders finally started to shake. Then her whole body slumped against the door. It swung open, and she disappeared into the locker room.

Emmy could barely focus for the rest of the match, and she wasn't the only one struggling. Everyone on the Wellsworth side seemed rattled. In the end they still won, but it was a lot closer than it should have been.

Emmy tried to find Lola after the match, but there was no sign of her. She must have gone back to the team bus, or maybe she went to hide in her mom's apartment for a while. Jack clambered down the stadium steps so fast Emmy was afraid he might fall.

"Did you see her anywhere?" he asked.

Emmy shook her head.

"I knew things were bad, but crikey, I thought at least her football team would like her."

"You should have heard the things they were saying about her on the pitch," Emmy said.

Jack's lip started wobbling. "We've got to get her out of there, Em. That place is going to kill her."

Emmy felt her face crumple. He was right. They had to get her out of there. She looked around and pulled Jack away from the crowd. "You're right. I need you to call Vincent."

Jack tipped his head to one side, suddenly looking more confused than upset. "Vincent? Like, my brother, Vincent?"

"Yeah. I need him to set up a meeting."

"With who?"

Emmy took a deep breath. "With Jonas."

Emmy stepped out of the car. King's Lynn was icy cold that morning, but that wasn't the only reason she was shaking.

Jack opened his car door.

"You've got to stay here," Vincent said from the driver's seat.

"Not bloody likely," Jack said.

"That wasn't a suggestion," Vincent said.

"I'm not letting her go out there alone with him."

Vincent laughed. "You think if the Order was planning something, you'd be able to stop them?"

"No." Jack tipped his chin and stared hard at his brother. "But at least she'd have somebody with her."

Vincent's face changed, and Emmy saw something in his eyes she'd never seen when he looked at his brother. Respect.

"It's okay, Jack," Emmy said. "Jonas isn't going to hurt me. He needs me."

"For now," Jack muttered as he slumped back down into the car.

Vincent stuck his head out the driver's window. "Head to the end of the car park and hop the brick fence. You can't miss it."

It was still early in the morning, so the parking lot was almost deserted. She stepped out of the way of a businessman who seemed to be in a terrible hurry for a Sunday morning. Emmy saw what she was looking for before she hopped the fence. Vincent was right; you couldn't miss the white stone gate.

The gate was actually red, although it had a few white bricks here and there, but she'd gotten used to the quirky place names in Britain. Calling it a gate was a bit of an exaggeration. It was really just an archway, the last remnants of an old abbey that had been destroyed five hundred years before. She leaned against the cold brick. Lucy had been livid when she'd told her she was going to King's Lynn again. She'd forbidden Emmy from going, said she was being selfish and didn't care if she ruined Lucy's life. Emmy didn't know how not making it into some club would ruin her life, and she didn't care. Lucy's reputation definitely didn't make the list of things Emmy was worried about these days.

She checked the time on her phone. She'd been waiting over twenty minutes. Vincent had said Jonas would be here, but maybe there'd been a change of plans. Maybe he'd left some kind of message for her instead.

She walked around the archway, but she didn't find any packages or notes. She stepped out onto the street to get a better look at the side. At the bottom of the arch was a plaque. She made sure no cars were coming, knelt down, and began to read.

Friar Aleyn. Was that how her family used to spell Allyn?

Emmy hugged her scarf around her neck. Who was this friar? Some long-lost ancestor of hers?

"An interesting man, that Friar Aleyn was."

Emmy's throat tightened. Even though she'd asked for the meeting, it didn't make hearing Jonas's voice any easier.

"Studied at Cambridge, was an expert in the writings of medieval mystics, and had a tendency to get himself into trouble with his superiors. Not unlike other Allyns I know." Jonas looked up at the top of the archway, as if he were a tourist who was curious about an old relic. "You're here alone, then?"

"Jack is in the car with Vincent."

Jonas nodded, and Emmy finally understood why he'd been so late. He'd been watching from somewhere close by, making sure she hadn't brought a teacher or some other adult with her.

"I hear you have some information for me."

Emmy swallowed. "No."

"No? I guess I'll just be going, then." He started to walk away.

"Hey, wait!" Emmy called after him. "I want to help you."

Jonas turned around. "I'm listening."

Emmy moved closer. "I can't tell you where my dad is because I really don't know. I've been trying to find out, but I can't even get in touch with him."

"Then you'll have to find another way."

"I can't." Emmy could hear the desperation in her own voice. "He's spent ten years making sure not a single soul knows where he is. He's not going to stop now."

"So, you're here to beg for mercy for poor Miss Boyd, are you?"

"No." Emmy glowered at him. "I know better than to ask *you* to do the right thing."

"I do the right thing for members of the Order. My loyalty is always to them. So, what can a thirteen-year-old girl offer the Order of Black Hollow Lane?"

"I can't tell you where my dad is, but I might be able to get whatever you want from him."

Jonas raised his eyebrows. "What makes you think he has something I want?"

"You're going to way too much effort just for revenge."

"Some people go to the ends of the earth for revenge."

"Not you. It's too emotional. You're more practical than that. More logical." She knew he'd see through her flattery, but it might still soften him a little. She needed him to be in a good mood. "Besides, it's like you said, your loyalty is to the members of the Order. Revenge doesn't get your members anything."

Jonas smiled. "You know me better than I could have imagined. You're right, this isn't just about revenge."

"Then what's it about? Maybe I can help."

"And in exchange, I make sure Miss Boyd is readmitted to Wellsworth?"

"That's right."

"That's an interesting proposition," he said, "one that I am definitely willing to entertain." He sat on the edge of the statue and looked at the birds flocking over the river. "I want the medallions."

Emmy's heart skipped a beat. She didn't dare say a word.

"You threw Brother Loyola's box out the window of the Round Tower Church last year, correct?"

Emmy nodded, even though it wasn't true.

"But there were only a few medallions in the box, is that also right?"

Emmy nodded again. That's what she'd told him last year, and she wasn't about to correct him now.

"Then there's only one person who can have the rest of them."

She still didn't say anything. Jonas thought her dad had most of the medallions, but he was wrong.

"Get me those medallions and your friend will be safe and sound at Wellsworth by the end of the week."

Emmy's fingers started twitching. She already had what he needed. She could get in Vincent's car right now, drive to London, and hand over the medallions. She wouldn't even have to betray her father. Except...

"Having the medallions means you can get into those vaults, right?"

Jonas didn't say anything. He didn't need to. Emmy already knew what would happen. The Order would have almost unlimited resources. They would gain power all over the country, and maybe even beyond, and everything they did would be about getting more power for their members. They didn't care who got in their way. Everybody else was expendable...and in danger.

"I'll have to think about it," Emmy said.

"Tell me," Jonas said, "how's your roommate these days?"

Emmy's hands started to shake. "It was the Order, wasn't it? You had somebody push her down the stairs."

Jonas rubbed his hand on the rough stone arch. "There were a lot of Aleyns who went through this gate to become Carmelite Friars. Did you know that?"

Emmy shook her head.

"They lived and worked and died at the abbey." He pointed down the street beside the gate. "And right down there, in the middle of Carmelite Terrace, is where they were all buried."

Emmy wrapped her arms around herself. The air seemed to have gotten chillier.

Jonas turned to face her. "It doesn't seem like you're getting the message, so let me make it clear. I hurt your friend. I hurt your roommate. Here's the next person on my list." He pulled a picture out of the pocket of his hoodie and handed it to her. "I've been pretty easy on your loved ones so far, but that ends now." He pointed to a woman in the photograph. "Get me what I want, or I'll bury her in Carmelite Terrace with all the other useless Allyns." He walked away.

Emmy stared at the photograph. It was a picture of her mother. She was at a book signing table, and she was taking a photo with a fan.

Except it wasn't a fan.

It was Jonas.

He was standing right next to her, smiling, like he was just another one of her readers.

Emmy's whole body was shaking. It wouldn't have been hard for Jonas to find her mom—all her appearances were listed on her website—but there was something about seeing him with her that made it hard to breathe. Jonas could get to her mom anytime he wanted. And if Emmy didn't get him what he wanted...

Part of her wanted to call him back, to tell him everything right now.

She looked down the street, but Jonas had already disappeared.

Chapter 15

The Not-So-High Road

Emmy felt like she was stumbling all the way back to the car. *Stay calm. Vincent doesn't need to know how rattled you are.*

"So?" Jack asked as she got in.

Emmy didn't even look at him. "Can you drop us off at Lola's house?" she asked Vincent.

Vincent rolled his eyes. "I'm not a taxi, you know. I can't wait around all day while you play with your little friends."

"We'll find our own way back." It was Sunday, and Lola's mom had been spending most weekends in King's Lynn. Hopefully they could catch a ride back with her that night.

"What happened?" Jack whispered. "Are you okay?"

"Later," she muttered.

Emmy guided Vincent to Lola's apartment. They were about to get out when Vincent turned around and faced the back seat. "Listen, if Jonas is giving you a way out of whatever mess you two have gotten yourselves into, you'd better take it. That chance might not come around again." His face seemed softer than usual, and more genuine. It sounded like he didn't know what Jonas was doing. Or maybe he did, but he didn't like it much.

Emmy nodded. She and Jack walked into the cobbled court-yard, where the door to number three was already open wide. Lola was standing at the bottom of the steps, still wearing her pajamas.

"You got my text?" Jack asked.

Lola snorted. "No, I just like standing in the rain in my jimjams. Would you get upstairs already?"

They followed her up the narrow steps and into the little flat, where her dad was sitting at the kitchen table.

"Morning, Mr. Boyd," Emmy and Jack both said.

"How are you, sir?" Emmy asked.

He waved his hand dismissively. "Ask me after I've had my coffee, kids."

Emmy and Jack both smothered a smile and disappeared into Lola's room. They sat down on her bed, and Lola stared at them with her hands on her hips.

"What the bloody hell have you been doing? Why didn't you tell me that you were meeting with Jonas?"

"Because we knew you'd be mad," Emmy said.

"Of course I'm mad! How can you even think about working with him?"

"Because you're drowning out here!"

Lola blinked. "What does that have to do with Jonas?"

"Don't ask me," Jack said. "She won't tell me anything."

Emmy looked at Jack, then back at Lola. They needed to know how much danger they were in.

"It's not a coincidence that people don't like you at Erindale," Emmy said. "The Order is getting people to spread rumors about you and bully you. Those girls who jumped you got paid to do it."

Lola's jaw practically hit the floor. "They got paid?"

Emmy nodded. "I don't know how many people they've paid off, but enough to make sure your life is totally miserable."

Lola shook her head and mouthed something Emmy couldn't make out. Then her whole face broke into a huge grin. "YES!!!" She jumped up and pumped her fists in the air.

"Uh…" Emmy looked at Jack.

"I think she's finally lost it," he said.

"No, no," Lola said, "don't you get it? That means it's not my fault! They don't hate me because I'm too loud or too bossy or because I'm just an unlikable person." Her smile got even wider. "Actually, I'm so likable that you have to *pay* people to get them to hate me!" She laughed maniacally, and Emmy and Jack both joined in. A bit of hysterical laughter felt pretty good.

"So," Lola said once she'd started to calm down, "how are we going to beat the Order this time?"

All the happiness inside Emmy melted away. How *were* they going to beat them? Was that even possible?

"You're not the only target anymore." Emmy showed them the picture and Lola swore. "He's after anyone who's close to me."

"Except me," Jack said. "I think I'm pretty safe because of my family."

"Why does Jonas want your dad so badly?" Lola asked.

"It's not about my dad." Emmy swallowed hard. "I mean, Jonas thinks it is, but I already have what he wants."

Jack and Lola both stared at her, their eyes wide.

"He wants the medallions."

Lola shuffled onto the bed. "Does he know you still have them?"

"He still thinks I threw the box into the sea, but I told him there were only a few medallions inside. He thinks my dad still has the rest." Her chest shuddered as she took a deep breath. "So, I wouldn't even have to give up my dad. I could just give Jonas the medallions right now and everyone would be okay."

"Emmy, you can't be serious," Jack said.

"Yeah," Lola said, "you can't let him win."

"This isn't about winning." Emmy pulled at her hair. "He's going to start hurting the people I love. He's already hurting you, Lola, and it's going to get worse. Way worse." Tears spilled onto her cheeks. "I need to keep you safe. I need to keep my *mom* safe." She slumped into an armchair that was covered in laundry. Anger flared inside her again. She wished she'd never learned about the Order. She wished her dad had never gotten her involved in all of this. Then her family would be safe.

Jack stared at his hands. "You're right, Em. It is going to get worse. But that's nothing compared to what it would be like if he got those medallions." He gave her a grim look. "You think everyone would be safer then? Imagine the kind of power

195

they could have if they were the wealthiest organization in the country. Imagine how they could bribe people *outside* the country. Every quid they spent would be about getting stronger, and if they're willing to do this to thirteen-year-old kids, imagine what kinds of things they'd do if they didn't have to worry about getting caught."

Emmy didn't want to imagine that. They already worked like some kind of mafia. The thought of a mafia with well-respected members and endless amounts of money was pretty terrifying. "I wonder what his endgame is?" Lola said.

"His endgame?" Jack asked.

"Yeah, like, what's his plan for the money in all those vaults? What's his long-term goal?"

Emmy shrugged. "Beats me. Last year he said that the Order had opened those vaults in times of great need, and that this was one of those times."

"Do you think they've got some kind of money trouble?" Lola asked.

"I don't think so," Jack said. "I'm pretty sure a lot of the sales my dad and Vincent make are actually for the Order, and they've been raking it in lately, especially with Malcolm helping them now."

"I got the impression that Jonas wants to do some kind of

major expansion project," Emmy said. "I don't know what it is, but anything that gives the Order more power can't be a good thing." She leaned her head on the side of the chair. She was sick of the Order messing around in her life. She was sick of her *dad* messing around in her life. She felt like a giant tennis ball being sent back and forth between them, getting whacked on the head with every hit.

No. She wasn't going to be some kind of chess pawn that only moved when other people told her. It was time to fight back. "What Sam's doing isn't working. Brynn's never going to give up that secret."

"Then what do we do?" Jack asked.

She tapped her fingers on the arm of the chair. "If we can't get them to admit doing something illegal, we'll just have to *catch* them doing something illegal."

"And then what?" Jack asked.

"And then we blackmail them."

Lola and Jack looked completely gobsmacked, but Emmy didn't care. If the Order was going to fight dirty, so would she.

Chapter 16

The Next Move

Lola was spending the afternoon with her mom, so Jack and Emmy went for a walk. The morning fog had mostly lifted, so they cut across the train tracks and into the big park nearby known as "The Walks." They were walking past a strange red tower that seemed to sit in the middle of nowhere when Emmy's phone rang.

"Hello?"

"Hi, darling!"

"Hey, Mom." It was a huge relief to hear her mom's voice after seeing that picture of Jonas by her side.

"How's your weekend been so far?"

"Okay, I guess. How about you?"

"Okay. I'm in California doing some interviews, and, you know, it's always nice in California." She laughed, but it wasn't her usual laugh. It was high and tense.

"Is something wrong?" Emmy asked.

Her mother paused. "I spoke to Lucy last night."

Emmy twisted her fingers together.

"She told me that there had been an…an incident at a soccer match. Where that friend of yours was kicked off the field for some pretty serious behaviour issues. She also said that you insisted on going to King's Lynn even though you weren't allowed. Emmeline, I thought I made it clear that Lucy is in charge of you while you are in England. Disobeying her is unacceptable."

"The only reason she thinks it's a problem is because there are these people spreading rumors at one of their clubs," Emmy said. "They're saying things about me and Lola that aren't true."

"Emmy, I'm sorry, but that's completely ridiculous. Why would a group of grown adults spread rumors about children?"

Emmy didn't say anything. She couldn't explain the Order to her mom. She brushed a tear off her cheek. "Lucy doesn't actually care about me. All she cares about is getting into some stupid club. I don't even know why it's so important to her."

Her mom sighed. "Listen, I didn't tell you this earlier because it's honestly none of your business, but Lucy and Harold were involved in, well, a scandal a few years ago. Harold was accused of insider trading, and some people at one of his clubs helped clear him of the charges. He might not have been found innocent without those friends."

Emmy couldn't help but feel for Lucy. It must have been scary to have your husband accused of a crime.

"Even though he was found innocent, their reputation took a huge hit. He had a tough time finding clients, and I think it's taken a while for them to feel stable again. I'm sure you can understand how stressful it is to think that their reputation is being threatened again."

"Look, I'm sorry about what happened to them," Emmy said, "but it's not my fault. And it's not Lola's fault, either."

"Emmy, she stole money from a charity, and—"

"She didn't steal it!"

"—and she's consistently shown that she has a violent temper. How can you continue to defend her?"

"She's my best friend," Emmy said simply.

"I don't know what kind of hold this girl has on you," her mom said, "but it isn't healthy. Instead of going to King's Lynn next time you have a free weekend, I'd like you to spend a weekend with Lucy."

"Why?"

"I think it would be good for you to connect with some people outside of school. There's more to life than just school friends."

That was easy for her mom to say. She didn't know that Emmy's school friends were in danger. Her mom didn't know *she* was in danger. Emmy bit her lip. Maybe she should tell her mom about Jonas's threats. That way she'd be on her guard. But then she'd pull Emmy out of Wellsworth for sure, and she'd never see her friends again. Besides, it probably wouldn't make her any safer. Jonas would always be able to find her.

"I'll go see Lucy," Emmy mumbled. She didn't want to fight with her mom right now.

"Thank you. I love you, Em. I know you care about this Lola girl, but I have to keep you safe."

Keep her safe. That's what Barlowe said. That's what her dad said. Everybody talked about keeping her safe, but it wasn't working. All they were doing was making it harder for her to keep everybody else safe.

Emmy rubbed tears onto her sleeve. "I love you too, Mom. You be safe too, okay?"

"I will, darling."

Emmy shoved her phone back in her pocket. "I guess you caught all that?" she asked Jack.

He nodded. "The Order really knows what they're doing, huh," he added quietly.

"Yup," Emmy sniffed. "I still don't get why they're harassing Lucy and Harold, though. All they've managed to do is to get Lucy to bug me about what I'm doing all the time. Why would they…"

Emmy stopped walking. "That's how they're tracking me."

"What do you mean?"

"That's how the Order knows what I'm doing all the time! Think about it: the only person who knows where I am, what societies I've joined, and what marks I'm getting is Lucy. And the only reason she knows—"

"—is because they convinced Lucy that she needs to keep a close eye on you so she'll get into the Thackery Club," Jack finished.

"But how would they get all those details from her?" Emmy asked.

"Maybe they've got some kind of tracker on her phone."

Emmy smacked her forehead. "The first time I met Lucy she said some club members had given them a deal on cell phones. I bet those phones had trackers in them so they could read her text messages. They might even be able to hear her phone calls!"

Jack looked sick to his stomach. "Are you sure going after the Order is a good idea?"

"No," Emmy admitted, "but I'm not going to sit around and wait for them to hurt the people I love. We need to beat them at their own game."

Jack breathed out and looked at the sky. "All right. So how do we do that?"

That was a good question. The Order had been keeping secrets for hundreds of years, and they'd gotten really, really good at it.

"Who do we know who's part of the Order?" Emmy asked.

"Well, there's Brynn, Larraby, and Jonas," Jack said, "and then my family."

Emmy winced. Jack's family would be the most logical people to spy on, because Jack wouldn't even need to come up with an excuse. He was *supposed* to be in his own house.

"I know what you're thinking, Em." Jack looked down at the grass. "But I don't know if I can spy on my own family."

"No," Emmy said, "of course not." Jack had enough trouble with them as it was. She couldn't ask him to betray them like that, even if he didn't like the things they were involved in.

"Okay." Jack looked relieved. He never seemed to know what to do about his family, and Emmy didn't want to make that worse. "I guess that leaves Brynn, Larraby, and Jonas."

Emmy turned around to make sure no one was following them. There was a couple walking under the willows, a few tourists by the old red tower, and a man reading a book on a bench. None of them were close enough to eavesdrop.

"Well, Jonas is out," Emmy said. "We don't even know where he is most of the time, and even if we did, it's not like he wouldn't notice us."

"We've already got Sam working on Brynn," Jack said. "He's really the only person who has a chance of getting anything out of him."

"If he's even trying anymore," Emmy mumbled. He hadn't even talked to her since that day outside humanities class.

"He is," Jack assured her. "I know we don't see him a lot, but that's part of the plan."

"But you're his roommate," Emmy said. "Shouldn't you be seeing him and talking to him and checking in all the time?"

"We do talk," Jack said. "Sometimes it's about Brynn, but

mostly it's other stuff. It's nice to just, you know, be friends. And not be obsessing about the Order all the time."

Emmy nodded. She wished she didn't have to obsess about the Order all the time. "Well, we'd better figure out how to get to him soon. Jonas's patience isn't going to last much longer."

They spent over a week watching Larraby as much as they could. Neither of them had classes with him, which made it a lot harder. They sat near his table at every meal, they stayed close during house study sessions, and Emmy even made up an excuse to get help from him in his office. By Tuesday, they had only found out one useful thing, but it was a very useful thing—Larraby was not careful with his phone.

"You're sure the passcode's 1493?" Emmy asked as she sliced through a piece of asparagus. They had managed to find a table to themselves in the Hall where it was loud enough to not be overheard.

"Pretty sure," Jack said.

"*Pretty* sure? Yesterday you said you were 100 percent sure!"

"It's either 1493 or 1463, but I'm pretty sure he pushed the nine."

Emmy rubbed her forehead. There were way too many things that could go wrong with this plan. If you could even call it a plan.

"You'll grab your purse after supper, right?" Jack asked.

"Yeah, but I still think that's a dead giveaway, 'cause I never carry a purse."

"Larraby doesn't know that."

They finished their plates and hurried back to the common room. Both of them went up to their rooms and grabbed their school books for study session. Emmy grabbed the great big handbag her mom had gotten her for Christmas and stuffed it with as many knickknacks as she could. They met back down in the common room, where they spread their books across a table, being careful to take up an extra spot. Then they waited.

Emmy tapped her pencil on the table. What if Larraby didn't show up? That wouldn't exactly be unusual. What if he didn't have his phone with him? They had already spent a whole week just watching him, which didn't leave much time to actually execute their plan. If it didn't work tonight, they'd have to wait until the next study session, or maybe even the one after that. Jonas could go after her mom any day now.

People started trickling in from dinner. Sam came in by himself. His hair was back to being scruffy. He looked at her and she started to smile. Then she remembered she was supposed to hate him. She tightened up her jaw and looked down at the table. When she looked back up, he was sitting next to Brynn.

Somebody leaned on the table next to Emmy. It was Victoria.

"Told you that boy was trouble," she said with a smug smile.

Emmy didn't say anything. She couldn't wait to tell Victoria, to tell everybody that it had all been an act. Except she wasn't so sure it was an act anymore.

The common room was just about full, which was exactly what they were hoping for. Oliver came down the stairs carrying a stack of books that seemed too big for such a small boy.

"Can I sit there?" he asked, pointing to the empty seat between Jack and Emmy.

Jack's face fell. "Sorry, Oli, we need this spot for somebody else."

"Oh, okay." Oliver shuffled to another empty spot, his ears bright red.

"Shoot," Jack said, throwing a worried glance at Oli's slumped back. "I hate doing that to him."

"We'll make it up to him when this is all over." *If* it was ever over.

Madam Boyd came out of her office and everyone started working. Emmy read the same sentence three times. Where was Larraby?

Fifteen minutes later he sauntered through the door, waving to his favorite students like it was normal for a teacher to be late.

Jack breathed out hard. "Ready?"

Emmy fiddled with the zipper on her purse. "I guess so."

Jack cracked his neck, got up, and walked over to Larraby. Emmy couldn't hear them, but she knew what Jack was saying. Larraby looked puzzled. Jack never asked him for help.

Finally, he followed Jack to their table. Jack walked ahead of him and sat in the same chair so Larraby had to sit in between him and Emmy.

"I'm really confused, sir," Jack said. "I've never conjugated anything in pluperfect tense before."

"I'm surprised your teacher hasn't been more thorough," Larraby said as he pulled his chair closer.

They talked through Jack's worksheet and Emmy pretended to be absorbed in her work. Jack shook his head. "I'm sorry sir, but Master Criggs told us the first-person ending was 'ero', not 'eram.'"

"Well, it's 'eram,'" Larraby said irritably.

Jack bit his lip. "Do you think you could look it up online? I just want to make sure I can prove to Master Criggs that I'm right."

"Fine," Larraby pulled out his phone and started tapping. Then he showed it to Jack. "See?"

Jack leaned in close and squinted at the phone. "Great, thanks." He moved his textbook closer so there was no space between the two of them. "I was also really confused by this section here."

Emmy held her breath. *Don't put it back in your pocket, please don't put it back in your pocket.*

Larraby looked at the textbook and put his phone down on the table. It was still pretty close to his body. He'd definitely notice if Emmy snatched it. She needed her distraction to work.

Emmy stood up and grabbed the handbag from the wrong end. Then she wrapped her foot around Larraby's chair and flung herself forward. She careened into Larraby and the purse burst open, spilling knickknacks all over the table.

"Oh my gosh," she said, "I'm so sorry!" She started shoving things into her purse, sweeping them in quickly like she was horribly embarrassed.

"Quite all right, dear." Larraby pushed his chair back to give her more space and Emmy reached for something that had landed close to Jack. With her body covering her left hand, she picked up the phone and slid it into the purse.

She grabbed the last of the items and swung the bag over her shoulder. "Sorry."

"So, when do I use pluperfect tense again?" Jack asked as he pointed to his textbook.

Emmy never heard the answer. She went straight up the stairs and into her room before pulling Larraby's phone out of her bag.

"One-four-nine-three," she whispered as she punched the numbers onto the keypad.

Larraby's phone came to life.

Emmy's fingers tingled as she tapped on the email icon, clicked the search button, and typed in "Black Hollow Lane."

No results.

She tried "Brother Loyola." Nothing.

When she typed in "Order" about a hundred emails came up, but none of them seemed to have anything to do with the Order of Black Hollow Lane.

Her lip started quivering. Larraby could notice his phone was gone any minute now. Maybe he used a different email address for things about the Order, or maybe they didn't even use email. It might be too traceable.

She tried "Jonas" and "Thomas Allyn," but nothing came up. She bit her lip. There was one more name she could try. She said a silent apology to Jack and typed in the name "Galt."

A handful of emails came up. She started at the bottom and read every one of them, but there was nothing specific, no details that indicated anything illegal.

She felt her shoulders slump. She should have known they'd never put anything like that in writing.

She clicked on the most recent email and started to read:

> Everything is arranged for the British Library event. BL will be in touch with further instructions. I have attached a list of the documents to be displayed so you can be prepared for conversation. Don't be late.
>
> D. Galt

Emmy's heart skipped a beat. Could "BL" be Brother Loyola? She didn't have time to think about it now. She whipped out her own phone and took a picture of the email and attachment. Then she shoved both phones back in the purse and walked downstairs.

Jack was still asking a very bored-looking Larraby

questions. Emmy sat down, put the bag under the table, and tossed the phone under Larraby's chair. Then she went back to her reading.

Jack didn't let up on Larraby until study session was done. When Larraby pushed back his chair, Emmy looked down.

"Is that your phone, sir?" She pointed under his chair.

"My goodness, yes, thank you." He picked it up and hurried away. He looked thoroughly relieved to be leaving their table.

Emmy and Jack packed up their things quietly. It was too close to curfew to go outside and talk.

Jack put his bag on his shoulder. "Get anything?" He didn't dare ask anything more specific.

"I think so," Emmy said. "At least, I hope so."

Chapter 17

The Socialite Comes Through

E mmy filled Jack in at lunch time the next day.

"Did you look up anything about this British Library event?" he asked.

She nodded. "They have a list of events on their website, but I don't know which one the tickets are for."

"Maybe that list of documents will help us figure it out."

They wolfed down the rest of their lunch and raced to the

library. They sat at a computer desk that was far away from everyone else. Emmy didn't think anyone had followed them, but she wasn't going to take the chance that someone could hide in the stacks and overhear them. She pulled out her phone while Jack found the British Library website.

"Looks like they've got a couple of events every week." Jack looked over her shoulder at her phone. "What kind of documents were in the email?"

Emmy quickly scrolled down so he wouldn't see the sender's name. She hadn't told Jack that his dad was the one who had sent the email. It was awkward enough for her to read it, let alone for his son.

"There's Matthew Paris's *Map of Britain*, the *Anglo-Saxon Mappa Mundi*, *Tournai Map of Asia*—"

"It's got to be the medieval map event," Jack interrupted. He clicked on a link and began to read:

Patrons may join us on December 6 for an exclusive, one-night exhibit of a long-forgotten collection of medieval maps. In addition to our own maps, we are featuring *The Alnwick Collection*, named for its recent discovery in Alnwick Castle, which includes five stunning maps on loan from a private collector. Of special interest are two previously unknown maps, the *Abbasid Caliphate* and *The Plan of Springs at Blacehol Abbey*.

Emmy clamped her hand over her mouth. Blacehol Abbey. That's what Wellsworth was before it was turned into a school. "The Order must be after that document."

Jack nodded. "I wonder what it is."

The first bell rang, telling them they had five minutes to get to their next class. They both jammed their things into their backpacks.

"Text Lola," Emmy said. "Her lunch break is later than ours. Get her to look it up if she's got time."

They ran off in opposite directions and didn't see each other until humanities, which was always their last class of the day.

"Did you hear back?" Emmy asked as she slid into the seat next to Jack.

Jack nodded. "She says we should call her after class."

Emmy had rarely been so distracted in one of Master Barlowe's classes. What was this "plan of springs"? It must be a map—all the other documents were—but what kind of map was it? And what did the Order want with it?

She was so lost in thought that the bell made her jump.

She and Jack didn't have to say anything to each other. They packed up their things and headed straight for the mud flats.

Jack pressed the video call button, and Lola quickly appeared on the screen.

"I found the document," Lola said.

Emmy bounced on her toes. "What is it?"

"It *says* that it's a map of some underground springs where the monks could access water," Lola said, "but I don't think that's actually what it is. The archivists who cataloged it were surprised at how many springs were mapped, and how intricately the monks laid the pipes to reach them. Almost like they were building tunnels."

Emmy and Jack stared at each other. *Tunnels.* They had been in those tunnels just last year. Those tunnels were called Black Hollow Lane, and they were a hideout for the Order.

"Are you saying there's a map of Black Hollow Lane at the British Library?" Jack asked with a crackling voice.

"I think so. The map's from the fifteenth century, so I'd imagine the tunnels weren't nearly as big back then. I bet the Order's been expanding them ever since the monastery was dissolved and the school took over."

"Did you find a picture of the map?" Emmy asked.

"No, it was only discovered a few months ago. It was stuffed inside a book at Alnwick Castle. This exhibition will be the first time it's being displayed. I read an article that said the person who owns this collection is very private, and he's not planning to let it out in public again anytime soon."

"Did it say who the collector is?" Jack asked.

Lola shook her head. "I don't know what the Order wants with the map, though. I mean, they already know everything about the tunnels, don't they?"

Emmy felt a tingling on the back of her neck. "They don't know everything."

"What do you mean?" Jack asked.

"Barlowe told me that there used to be a way to get to the vaults without using medallions, but that it was blocked by cave-ins and nobody knows exactly where the oldest passageways are." She looked at Lola. "When did you say this map was made?"

"The fifteenth century," Lola said. "That's a hundred years before the monastery was even dissolved, so these are definitely the oldest tunnels."

"If this is a map of the oldest tunnels..." Jack said.

"...then it's a map to the vaults," Emmy said. "One that doesn't need medallions." Her pulse started thudding in her ears. If the Order got ahold of this map, then everything they'd done to keep the medallions safe would be for nothing.

From what Jonas had told her, there were millions of dollars' worth of artifacts inside them, maybe tens of millions. The idea of the Order having that kind of money was terrifying.

"We've got to stop them," Jack said.

"How?" Lola said.

Nobody said anything. How could they stop an organization that was so strong?

"We can't," Emmy said quietly.

"We can't stop them. They're always ten steps ahead of us."

"Then what are we supposed to do?" Lola asked, throwing her hands in the air. "Just let them take it and be on their merry way?"

"We can't stop them," Emmy said, "but maybe we can *catch* them. If we can get proof that they're trying to steal it, we can take that to Jonas and force him to back off of taking the map and off of Lola and my family."

"Oh, good," Lola said, "we only have to catch them, and then we can take Jonas out for tea afterward and convince him to be a good bloke. Sounds bloody easy."

"Jonas'll never be a good guy," Emmy said. "We just have to convince him that he has more to lose than we do."

"We'll have to catch them first," Jack said. "How are we supposed to do that?"

"We'd need some kind of surveillance equipment," Lola said. "That's the only way we'll get proof."

"Sam might be able to help us with that," Emmy said. "He might know about different cameras and stuff."

Jack ran his hand through his hair. "Do you think we should tell Sam what's going on?"

"Why?" Lola asked. "I thought we said it was too risky."

"That was before Jonas threatened to go after anyone close to Emmy. I mean, if Brynn figures it out and tells Jonas that Sam's been spying on the Order for us, that's going to put a big target on his back."

Emmy brushed her hair out of her face. Jonas couldn't possibly know that Emmy got a swooping feeling in her stomach every time Sam smiled at her. He couldn't know that her cheeks felt hot when she thought about Sam for too long. But if he found out Sam was spying for Emmy, he'd know they were friends, and that would be enough to put him at risk.

"Okay," Emmy said, "we'll tell him when we ask for the cameras."

"We've got to figure out how we can get into the event first," Jack said. "It's a preview opening, so not just anyone can go. You'd probably have to be a big donor or something."

"There's got to be some socialite who just gives loads of cash so they can be prestigious," Lola said, "someone who wouldn't actually be interested in using their tickets."

Emmy pressed her lips together. A London social climber who only cared about reputation. "I think I know someone."

Emmy waited until after dinner to make the call. She wasn't exactly looking forward to it.

"Hello?" said a surly voice on the other end of the phone.

"Hi Lucy, it's Emmy."

"I know who it is," Lucy snapped. "I know how to use a smartphone. So, what kind of trouble are you in now?"

"I'm not in any trouble," Emmy said. "My mom told me to call you and arrange a time to come stay for the weekend."

Lucy moaned. She didn't seem any happier about this idea than Emmy did.

"I was hoping to come the weekend of December sixth. There's this event at the British Library that I want to go to, and I was hoping you could get me some tickets."

"Can't you get them yourself?"

"It's a preview of a special exhibit, so I can't just order the tickets online."

"Why do you need to go to a preview? Can't you just wait and see the exhibit like everybody else?"

Emmy crossed her fingers. "I'm competing for an award in the Medieval Society. It's one of the most prestigious awards in the school."

Lucy was silent. Emmy finally had her attention.

"If I do a presentation about the exhibition before anyone else gets a chance to see it, that'll really boost my chances of winning. I'd tell *everybody* about how my amazing cousin got me those super-exclusive tickets." She crossed her fingers even tighter. "I bet everyone at the Thackery Club would love to hear how you turned a troublemaking girl into an academic award-winner."

Lucy paused. "You're laying it on a bit thick, aren't you?"

"I'm just making sure you know the full situation…and how it might affect your reputation."

Emmy heard a clicking sound, like Lucy was rapping her fingernails on a table. "How many tickets do you need?"

Chapter 18

The Spy, Revisited

Emmy's shoes squelched as she hopped from one patch of soggy grass to the next. The tide at the mud flats must have been high that afternoon. Even the shore was waterlogged.

"What time is Sam supposed to be here?" Emmy asked.

"Five," Jack said. "Let's hope he's ready for this."

"Ready to hear that a secret society might come after him if they find out who his friends are?" Emmy laughed. "Nobody's ready for that."

The sun was already setting behind the cliffs, and all the warmth of the day was disappearing with it. Emmy rubbed her stocking-covered legs, wishing she'd worn the slacks that came with her uniform instead of the skirt.

Footsteps crunched on the forest path. Emmy closed her eyes and tried to ignore the nerves that gurgled in her stomach. Time to tell Sam the truth.

But when a boy came out of the trees, it wasn't Sam. It was Oliver.

"Oli, what are you doing here?" Jack asked.

Oliver pulled at the sleeves on his sweater. "I saw you guys going for a walk, and I thought I'd come with you."

Emmy's fingers twitched. Oliver couldn't see Sam with them. Everyone needed to think Sam hated them, otherwise he wouldn't be safe.

"This isn't a good time," Jack said. "I mean, we just need to be on our own for a bit."

Oliver blinked a few times, then looked back and forth between them. "Oh, sorry," he mumbled. "I thought you guys were just friends."

Jack looked horrified, which was pretty much how Emmy felt, too.

"Ew, gross!" Jack said. "No offense, Emmy, but—"

"No, totally gross," Emmy said. "We are absolutely, positively, definitely just friends. We just, um…" How were they going to think up a plausible excuse to get rid of Oliver without making him think she was Jack's girlfriend?

"Lola asked us to call her," Jack said, "and she said it was something serious. She just, you know, needs her privacy and all."

Oliver nodded and ducked his head. "Sorry I bothered you." He went back up the path, his shoulders bent over like they were being pressed by some invisible weight.

"We'll hang out later, okay?" Jack called.

Oliver didn't turn around.

Jack ran his fingers through his hair. "Now he thinks I don't want to be around him."

"He's still having a hard time, isn't he?"

"I think so. I haven't seen him hanging around with a lot of first years, and he doesn't seem that happy here." He looked up at the sky. "I don't know what to do, though. I can't make people be friends with him, and I can't be with him twenty-four-seven. I just… I don't know. I just hope he's okay."

A twig snapped close by and they both looked up. Sam came out of the forest, a lopsided smile on his face. Emmy felt the familiar swoop in her stomach, but this time she wasn't sure if it was just from nerves.

"Did anyone see you?" Jack asked.

"I passed your brother on the path."

Emmy cringed. "He knows we're out here."

"Don't worry," Sam went on. "I pulled out my phone and muttered something about it being impossible to get a signal around here. Hopefully he thought I was just trying to find a decent place to use my mobile. So, what's going on? You said you need some kind of tech help?"

"Yeah," Jack said heavily, "but there's something else we need to talk about, too."

"Let's do the tech stuff first. It sounds like I'll like that part best."

"We need to be able to, um, catch someone doing something wrong," Jack said.

"Aren't you already trying to catch Brynn?"

"This is a bit, um, different," Emmy said. "We need some kind of cameras. Really small ones that we can, like, wear or something, but nobody else can see them."

Sam kicked a rock out of the mud. "All right, what's going on? Like, for real this time. 'Cause secretly filming people's pretty creepy."

"It's nothing like that," Emmy said. "I mean, I guess it kind of is, but it's not for a creepy reason."

Sam stared at both of them like they might be losing their minds.

Jack looked at Emmy. "I think we'd better tell him the second part."

Emmy pressed her lips together. How were you supposed to start a conversation where you were going to tell someone they were in danger? And that you were the one who had *put* them in danger?

"We have to tell you something," Jack said. "Something that maybe we should have told you a while ago, but, well…"

"It's kind of complicated," Emmy said.

Sam crossed his arms across his chest. His smile was long gone.

"There's a reason Brynn framed Lola," Emmy said.

"If it was really him," Sam muttered.

"It really was him, but it wasn't just about getting her expelled." Emmy closed her eyes and tucked her hair behind her ear. "Brynn is part of a secret society. A really nasty one."

Sam's forehead crinkled, but he didn't say anything.

"They're called the Order of Black Hollow Lane, and last year, their leader tried to kill me."

Sam looked at Emmy, then at Jack. Then he let out an awkward laugh. "Yeah right. I'm not falling for that."

"It's true," Jack said. "They recruit people here at Wellsworth, and they get involved in all kinds of illegal stuff once they leave school."

"How do you know that?" Sam didn't look like he believed them for a second.

"Because my dad and older brothers are part of it."

Sam cleared his throat. "Come on, guys, a joke's a joke, but trying to convince me that your family's a bunch of criminals and that someone's trying to kill a kid, that's a bit much."

"He's not trying to kill me right now," Emmy said. "He's trying to get me to do something for him in exchange for getting Lola back into Wellsworth."

"What's he trying to get you to do?" Sam looked more uncertain than skeptical now.

Emmy looked at Jack. "I can't tell you that. It's too dangerous."

Sam shook his head. "Right. I don't know what's going on with you two, but it's pretty weird." He turned around and walked back toward the path.

"Wait!" Emmy's shoes slipped in the mud. "Don't go yet!" He couldn't leave thinking they were just making up a story.

He might tell someone about it. "You know that skull that you have to press to get into Latin Society?"

Sam looked back. "What about it?"

"It's a skull with a cross on the right and a dagger on the left."

"So?"

"I bet you've seen it in other places, too. It's their symbol."

"Have you ever noticed Brynn disappearing in the evening?" Jack asked. "Making up some excuse and then disappearing for a few hours?"

"Yeah," Sam said, his eyes narrowing. "It happens a lot, actually."

"That's because he's going to meetings," Jack explained. "Meetings with the Order of Black Hollow Lane. We think Larraby runs the meetings here. That's why we wanted you to keep an eye on him."

"Their leader thinks I can get something that he really needs," Emmy jumped in. She needed to be vague about this part, but she had to give Sam enough details to make him believe her. "It's something that somebody in my family had, and he'll do pretty much anything to get it."

Sam took a few squelching steps toward them. "Why are you guys telling me this stuff?"

Emmy swallowed hard. "Because the leader of the Order is threatening my friends. He said if I don't do what he wants, the people I care about are going to be in danger."

"It's no accident that Lola's been having such a hard time at her new school," Jack said. "The Order is making sure people are as awful to her as possible. They even got a couple of girls to beat her up."

"This is wild," Sam muttered.

"Yeah, it is," Emmy said. "But it's true."

Sam rubbed his face. He was a lot paler than he'd been a few minutes before. "Why didn't you tell me this before?"

"At first we didn't know if the Order was involved," Jack said.

"Yeah, but you've known for a while, right?" Sam was pacing now, his hands slammed inside his pockets.

"We didn't think it would be good for you to know," Emmy said meekly.

"Good for me or good for you?" Sam snapped. "Did you think I'd chicken out if I knew it was dangerous?"

"No! And we didn't think it was dangerous for you, otherwise we wouldn't have asked!" Emmy could hear the desperation in her own voice. "We knew Brynn would be annoyed when he found out you were playing him, but we didn't think it was a big enough deal for the Order to care that much."

"And now?"

Emmy's eyes started filling up with tears. "And now...just being my friend is enough to put you in danger."

Sam laughed bitterly. "Friends? These are some pretty big secrets to be keeping from a friend."

Emmy wiped her cheeks with her sleeve, but more tears kept coming. She hadn't thought he'd be this upset. She'd never wanted to hurt him.

"We are your friends," Jack insisted. "That's why we're telling you this."

Sam ran his hand through his hair. His face was crumpled, like he was more than just angry. "I never would have done this if I'd known about Brynn."

"I'm sorry." Emmy's voice cracked. "I'm so sorry. We never meant to put you in danger."

"You don't understand," Sam said. He rubbed his face again, like he didn't know what to do. "I never would have..." His voice trailed off and he started muttering to himself. "What did I do? Did I say anything that... What did I do?"

"You can stop helping us," Emmy choked. "You can stop spying on Brynn."

"You don't get it!" Sam stopped pacing and whirled around at them. "I haven't been spying on Brynn!"

Emmy's breath seemed to get caught in her throat. She looked at Jack, whose face was wrinkled and confused.

"What do you mean?" he asked.

Sam bent over and put his hands on his knees. He didn't seem to be able to get enough air. Finally, he looked up. "I haven't been spying on Brynn. I've been spying *for* Brynn. I've been spying on you."

Chapter 19

The Truth Comes Out

E mmy felt like she'd been kicked in the gut. Sam couldn't be the spy. He just couldn't.

"Brynn came to me at the beginning of the year," Sam said. "He said that he wanted to pay me to spy on my roommate."

Jack's face didn't change. He stared blankly at Sam, like he didn't understand what he was hearing.

"He said you guys liked to mess around with each other. It seemed like it was just going to be for a laugh."

"You thought Lola being treated like dirt was all for a laugh?"

"I didn't think that had anything to do with Brynn. He wasn't on the footage, he was nowhere near that part of the school that night, and he swore up and down that he didn't do it."

"We told you over and over that it was him." Emmy's tears started all over again, but she wasn't sad or guilty this time. She was furious. "Why couldn't you have just trusted us?"

"I don't know," Sam said. "Why couldn't you have trusted me enough to tell me the truth?"

Emmy didn't know what to say to that.

"Look, I never would have done it if I didn't need the money so bad. My mum already took a second job, and she still might lose her flat."

Emmy looked away. She didn't know what it was like to have to help your mom with money. It had to be really tough. But it still didn't make what Sam did okay.

"I didn't know what Brynn was really doing," Sam said. "I didn't know you guys. I wasn't friends with you when he asked me. I knew Brynn was a snob, but who cares? As far as I knew, he was offering me money to help him with a prank."

"Getting someone expelled isn't a prank," Jack whispered. His lip was shaking, and Emmy knew it wasn't just from the cold wind.

"I told you, I didn't think Brynn had anything to do with that! I risked my neck breaking into the security office so I could help her, didn't I? If Brynn had shown up on the security footage, I would have turned on him straight away."

Something clicked into place in Emmy's brain. The security footage. Sam was right. It didn't show Brynn. But it did show someone else, someone they had completely dismissed.

"It was you," she whispered. "Brynn paid you to take that money and plant it in Lola's room."

Sam's eyes looked like they might pop right out of his head. "Of course not! I've been trying to help you figure out who did it."

"You were in and out of the conference room all night," Emmy said. "It would have been so simple for you to slip in after Lola locked the money in there."

"No, it wouldn't," Jack said. "Remember he left early? He wouldn't have had time to get the money box."

"Are you actually defending him?"

"No! I mean…" Jack rubbed his forehead. "I don't know." He looked like something inside him was breaking.

"Why would I have gotten you that security footage if it might have shown that I was guilty?" Sam said.

"It's a pretty good cover, don't you think?"

"Come on, Emmy, I would never do something like that."

Emmy looked at the ground. She didn't know what Sam was capable of anymore.

"I swear," Sam said, "all I did was tell Brynn some of the things you were up to. It didn't seem like there'd be much harm."

Emmy's heart started beating faster. "What did you tell him?"

Sam started pacing. "I don't know, lots of stuff. I told him that you'd asked me to spy on him, and he got a real kick out of that. He thought it'd be brilliant for us to pretend to be friends, so you'd think your scheme was working."

Emmy wrapped her arms around her stomach. No wonder Brynn had accepted Sam so quickly. It was all part of his plan.

"What else?" Jack asked.

"He asked me what you guys talked about, and if you were sneaking around at all. He asked if you ever talked about your homes and your families, just regular stuff that anyone could find out."

"Wait." Emmy's pulse started thudding in her ears. "Did he ask you about my dad?"

"Yeah, I think so."

The thumping sound got louder. "What did you tell him?"

Sam shrugged and shook his head, like he was trying to

remember. "Just that you didn't know him that well, and that you'd only heard from him a few times in the last couple years."

Jack buried his face in his hand, and Emmy closed her eyes. That's how Jonas knew she'd heard from her dad. That's why he was so sure she'd be able to track him down and why she was being dragged into this mess again. She felt sick. She didn't know what to say or what to do. All she knew was that she wanted to get as far away from Sam as possible.

She pushed her way past Sam and up the hill onto the grass.

"Emmy, wait!" Sam called.

She didn't turn around. She never wanted to look at him again.

Emmy felt like she was in a fog for the next few days. Thankfully, she didn't have too many classes with Sam, because every time she saw him, her eyes filled up with angry tears. When she was by herself, she cried even more. She used to imagine sitting in a quiet café with him or playing games together with Jack and Lola. Now she couldn't imagine this ache going away. Natalie had noticed something was wrong, especially when Emmy skipped a soccer practice, but Emmy couldn't talk about what happened. There were too many secrets in the story.

When Emmy texted Lola about what happened, her reply consisted mostly of swearing and promises to pummel Sam the next time she saw him. The hardest part was seeing Jack so torn up. Sam had been the first close guy friend he'd had in a long time. He told Emmy it was no big deal, but she knew he was lying. He'd barely talked in three days. As soon as classes were over, he went straight to his room. He'd even missed a painting workshop.

They were sitting in the common room one evening when Sam came up to them carrying a box.

"Hey," Sam said.

Emmy felt her back get tight, and she looked straight at Jack. "I think I'm going to turn in for the night."

"Wait." Sam sat across the table from them. "I know you guys are up to something."

Emmy folded her arms across her chest and kept staring at Jack. Hopefully Sam would take the hint.

"Those cameras that you needed…" Sam looked around the noisy common room and leaned closer. "Does this have something to do with that Order you were telling me about?" he whispered.

"Why do you want to know?" Emmy asked. "Want to sell us out to Brynn again?"

"I haven't even seen Brynn since you told me about the Order," Sam hissed.

"Why not?" Emmy asked. "Did he dump you once he realized he couldn't use you as his spy anymore?"

Sam pulled at his hair. "I told you, I never would have gotten involved with Brynn if I'd known what he was really like."

"Well, now you know."

"Right! So, all I want to do is help you."

"How am I supposed to believe that?" Emmy asked. "You lied to us, you spied on us, you set Lola up—"

"I told you, I didn't have anything to do with the White Stone Gate money."

"Then who did?"

"How should I know?" Sam exclaimed, exasperated.

"Keep your voices down," Jack warned.

Emmy glanced behind her. Nobody seemed to be interested in them. She looked back at Sam. "How am I supposed to trust you?"

"I don't know." Sam rubbed his forehead with both hands. "I don't know what I can do to make you trust me again. All I can tell you is that I didn't know what was really going on, and if I had, I never would have done it."

Emmy looked down at the floor. Part of her wanted to believe Sam. He really had seemed like a good guy. Then again, Jonas had seemed like a good guy, too. What if Sam was still playing them?

She shook her head. "You used us. I'm sorry your mom's having a hard time, but selling us out like that... I can't just get over it."

She pushed her chair away from the table.

"We used him too, you know," Jack said quietly.

"What do you mean?"

"We used him to spy on Brynn. We asked Sam to pretend to be *Brynn's* friend to get information out of *him*."

Emmy opened her mouth, but closed it just as fast. "That's different," she finally said.

Jack looked her straight in the eye. "Is it?"

She shuffled her feet.

"Look," Sam said, "I know it doesn't make up for what happened, but here." He put the box on the table.

"What's that?" Jack asked.

Sam glanced around again. "They're buttonhole cameras. I bought them online with the money I made from Brynn.

Attach them to your sweater or jacket, and they'll record everything you see. I can set them up for you if you like." Sam looked up at her, hopeful.

Emmy looked at Jack, and he nodded at her.

"Show Jack how to do it, and he can set it up himself."

Sam's face fell, but he nodded. Emmy got up and tried not to think about how disappointed he looked.

On December 6, Emmy tore off the soccer pitch the moment the whistle blew. It was the last match until after the holidays, and she didn't even care that the other team had won. All she could think about was getting to King's Lynn as fast as possible. She had the quickest shower of her life and headed out the locker room door before most of her teammates had even gotten off the pitch. She texted Jack while she ran across the freezing grounds. *He'd better be ready*, she thought.

She grabbed the overnight bag from her room, hoping the dress she'd stuffed inside it earlier wouldn't get crunched too badly. By the time she got back to the common room, Jack was waiting for her. And he wasn't alone.

"Hey," Sam said to her.

Emmy looked away. It was a lot harder to be mad at Sam after all the things Jack had said, but she definitely wasn't ready to be friends.

"I don't know what you guys are up to tonight, but…" Sam looked around the mostly empty common room. Most people were still at the match. "Is it safe? Are you going to be okay?"

Emmy looked into Sam's eyes. He really did seem worried about them. And that made it harder for Emmy not to be worried, too. She didn't want to think about all the things that could go wrong. Larraby would be there, and he wasn't *completely* clueless. He'd know they were up to something as soon as he saw them. What if he got them kicked out of the party? What if they couldn't catch Larraby doing anything wrong? And what if other, more dangerous Order members showed up? Larraby might be the least of their worries. She twisted her fingers around the strap of her overnight bag. "We'll be fine."

Sam swallowed hard and nodded. Emmy felt a pang of worry in her stomach, then tore her eyes away from him and headed for the door. The trip to King's Lynn felt longer than usual. Madam Boyd hadn't seemed suspicious when Emmy had said her cousin had invited them to London for the weekend. Lola was going to meet them at the King's Lynn train station, and they'd told both her parents that Lucy would meet them on the other end. Not that Lucy actually would. It wouldn't be the only time they bent the truth about this weekend.

Lola and her dad were waiting at the station. She said a quick goodbye to both her parents, who seemed keen not to spend much time in each other's presence. They found comfortable seats on the train, and Emmy tried to unclench some of the tension in her muscles. They had a two-hour train ride ahead of them, and her stomach couldn't handle so much adrenaline for that long.

"Everybody know what they're doing?" Lola said. Her voice was casual, like she was asking about their dinner plans.

"Yep," Jack said.

Emmy nodded, which felt like a lie. She knew what her job was tonight, but knowing what she was doing? That was a whole other story.

Chapter 20

The British Library

The walk from the station to the British Library was short, but it didn't feel like it.

"I thought it didn't snow in London," Emmy said, pulling her sweater tighter around her shoulders.

"It doesn't usually," Jack said. "At least it's not sticking."

"It's sticking enough to make me wish I didn't wear heels," Lola grumbled.

Emmy looked at Lola's shoes. "You call those heels? The back's barely higher than the front."

"Barely higher is still higher," Lola said.

They crossed the street, and Emmy brushed a few snowflakes out of her eyes. A tall, brick gate stood at the end of the block, and above it was a massive sign that read *British Library*. It made her want to turn around and just go back to Audrey House and sit by the nice warm fire...but that wasn't an option. Everyone she loved was depending on her. Thinking about that made her more determined and more terrified all at the same time.

The gate led to a wide courtyard that was surrounded by a sprawling, red building. The courtyard was slicker than the sidewalk, but they made it to the main entrance unscathed. The entrance hall was overwhelming, with seemingly endless hallways and staircases leading in every direction. There were desks beside each door with security guards looking in people's bags. Emmy resisted the urge to fiddle with the tiny camera poking out of her sweater's buttonhole. If the security guy saw it, their plan would be ruined before they even got inside.

He raised his eyebrows when he saw them. "You folks here for the medieval maps preview opening?"

They nodded and tried to look like they were supposed to be there.

The security guard looked them up and down, then pointed straight behind him. "Up the first set of stairs, then left around the next ones, and you'll find the gallery." They all scampered away from him as quickly as possible and walked up the stairs he'd pointed to. Music was playing from a room nearby. They went around the next flight of stairs and the music got louder, leading them toward a wide-open gallery filled with display cases.

A woman sat at a table in the doorway. "I'm sorry, this event is for ticket-holders only."

"They were set aside for us," Emmy said, "under the name Lucy Healey."

She narrowed her eyes at them. "You're Lucy Healey?"

"She's my aunt," Emmy said, which wasn't technically true, but it was close enough. "She said she would leave her phone number. You can call her if you need to."

The woman's shoulders relaxed. "That won't be necessary." Her hand hovered over all the different sets of tickets in front of her. "Here they are." She ripped them in half and gave each of them the torn ends. "Enjoy your evening."

They stepped into the gallery, which was already buzzing with people in glittering clothes. Emmy had never liked going to fancy parties with her mom but trying to catch a criminal at one was ten times worse. The camera in her buttonhole had felt so light and easy when she put it on. Now that she was actually at the exhibition, it felt twice as heavy, and it wouldn't stop scratching at her skin.

You know what to do, she said to herself. *You can get this done. For Lola. And for Mom.*

She closed her eyes and rolled her shoulders back. Time to catch some crooks.

"Remember to act natural," Lola said as she grabbed an egg roll off a passing tray. "What would you do if you were just a normal guest at a party like this?"

"Find a bathroom I could hide in until it's over," Emmy said, "or at least until my mom would come and drag me out."

Lola rolled her eyes. "Never mind."

"Let's go find the map," Emmy said, but Lola held onto her elbow.

"We can't all go," Lola said as she took another bite of egg roll. "It'll look suspicious if we all make a beeline for the item the Order wants to steal. I don't know if you've noticed, but three teenagers stick out like sore thumbs in this crowd."

Lola was right. The room was jam-packed with people now, but it still looked like they were the only ones under forty.

"You've got to look like you're having a good time," Lola

said, "like you're excited to get the chance to be at such a swanky party."

Jack tried to smile, but it looked more like the dentist had wired his teeth together.

Lola shook her head. "Emmy, you look for the map, and I'm going to teach Jack how to mingle with the old folks."

Emmy wandered past the heavy display cases that were woven around the room. She didn't find what she was looking for until she got to the very center, where two tall cases held the collection that was being displayed for the first time.

The Plan of Springs at Blacehol Abbey was crisp and clean. It had obviously been pressed inside that book where it was found. It was bigger than she expected and still showed crease lines from where it had been folded. Bright red lines and circles were drawn in every direction, like a giant maze without an exit. There were words, but they were all in Latin, just like every other document she'd seen. She smirked. No wonder they sent Larraby. A Latin teacher would have the perfect excuse for wanting to get a closer look at these maps.

There was a big red cross at the top with little dots decorating the tips. She didn't really understand what any of the symbols or images meant. Nothing looked that familiar, but then again, she'd only been in the tunnels once, and she had been running for her life. She didn't exactly make a mental map of where she'd been.

"Good evening, ladies and gentlemen!" The music stopped playing and a woman stood behind a podium on a little raised platform. "We are so glad you could join us for such a unique exhibition. These maps would still be hidden in the Alnwick Castle Library if it weren't for the tireless work of one man. He's one of the most prominent antiquities dealers in the country, and even though he acquired these maps for himself, he is graciously sharing them with us this evening. Please welcome the owner of the *Alnwick Collection*, Donovan Galt."

Emmy felt her jaw drop. It couldn't be. But Jack's father was walking up to the podium and shaking hands with the curator. Emmy looked around. Jack was ten feet away, staring at his dad like he was a stranger.

"What the bloody hell is this?" Lola had appeared next to Emmy. "He can't own the map. He's part of the Order. They wouldn't need to steal it if Donovan already had it."

Donovan leaned on the podium and smiled at the crowd. "Discovering this collection at Alnwick was a wonderful surprise. Some of the maps had particularly tricky inscriptions, which is why I needed the help of a Latin scholar to help date and authenticate them. He's going to share a bit about what we found. Please welcome Mr. Jameson Larraby."

Emmy whipped around and saw Larraby making his way through the crowd. She shook her head. Larraby had already seen the map. He'd helped authenticate it. He probably knew each tunnel inside and out.

Jack slipped through the crowd toward them. "What's going on? Why would they want to steal a map they already have?"

"They wouldn't," Emmy said. "They must not be planning on stealing it."

Larraby started talking about the inscriptions. It wasn't hard to tune him out.

"It doesn't make sense to bring it out in public," Jack whispered. "That just increases the chances that someone else will figure out what it is."

"But they *did* bring it out in public," Lola said. "There has to be a reason."

Larraby was still droning on. Emmy frowned. Donovan Galt wasn't listening, either. He was scanning the crowd, like he was looking for something. Or someone.

She started scanning too, and she wasn't the only one. There was at least one man at every door who was watching the crowd, eyes constantly moving, constantly searching. They were blocking the exits.

She felt Lola stiffen beside her. "There's somebody watching you. By the wall on your left, with a dark beard, carrying a brown satchel."

Emmy swallowed and turned her head. The man's eyes crinkled into a smile. She'd seen a sad smile like that before. On the face of a priest who wasn't really a priest.

She pressed two shaking fingers to her lips. There *was* someone else who might want a map like this. Not somebody who wanted to get the vaults' treasures for the Order, but who wanted to keep them *away* from the Order. Someone who would risk a lot for the chance to cripple the Order again.

She pushed past the other party guests until she reached him. "Does your absence still haunt you?"

The man gasped. He hadn't expected her to recognize him. Then his eyes filled with tears. "Every day."

Emmy felt her chin wobbling. All the things she'd imagined saying to her dad seemed to have evaporated. All she could do was stare.

If she hadn't been staring so intently, she might have seen them sooner. The men from the exits, moving slowly through the crowd. Moving toward them.

Emmy looked at Donovan. He wasn't scanning anymore. He was looking straight at Jack with a look of sheer panic on his face.

Something was about to happen, something he didn't want his son anywhere near.

Emmy didn't stop to think. She grabbed her dad's hand and pulled the red handle on the wall.

The fire alarm went off instantly.

The room was dead quiet for two seconds. Then it was pandemonium. Everyone started pushing for the exits. Emmy yanked her dad to the nearest one. Neither of them looked back at the men following them. Their only hope was that the crowd would slow them down.

They made it out the front doors, ignoring the security guard asking everyone to stay calm. The courtyard was covered in a thin layer of slush. Emmy and her dad slipped and slid toward the street. *Don't let go of his hand. Whatever happens, don't let go.*

"Taxi!" Emmy screamed before they'd even reached the sidewalk.

"Don't bother!" her dad yelled. He waved his hands and a car flew out of the theatre parking lot across the street. It sped across both lanes of traffic and screeched to a halt in front of them. Her dad pushed her inside and slammed the door shut behind them. The car burst to life and flew down the road.

"What happened?" asked the driver.

Emmy squinted at him and gasped. It was Master Barlowe.

"She spotted me," her dad said. "They were watching her pretty closely, so—"

"—so then they spotted you." Barlowe wrenched on the steering wheel and they careened onto a new street.

Emmy's dad yanked at his nose and a prosthetic came off, revealing his real nose underneath. He peeled off his fake beard and grabbed Emmy by both hands.

"It was a trap, wasn't it?" Emmy said to him. "They showed the map publicly so they could lure you out of hiding."

He nodded. "The map isn't even real, Emmy. It was all a big show."

His voice was quieter than she'd expected. More gentle. She wasn't sure if it triggered a memory buried deep inside her, or if just knowing it was her dad's voice was enough to make it feel right.

"If you knew the map was fake," she whispered, "why did you come?"

His eyes softened. "Nothing is more important to me than keeping you safe." He pulled his satchel off his shoulder and put a shaky hand to her cheek. "I didn't know what they would do tonight. I had to protect you."

The satchel was brown leather. Just like the one the teacher at Lola's school had. Just like the businessman in King's Lynn who seemed to be late for work on a Sunday.

"It was you. You've been following me all year."

"Margaret—or Madam Boyd, as you must call her—would let me know every time you'd be in King's Lynn. I knew Jonas would have someone following you. I had to be there. I had to make sure you were safe. I tried to help Margaret's daughter too, but it wasn't easy to get to her. At least I was able to get her locker moved out of that dark hallway."

Tears spilled onto Emmy's cheeks. She didn't even know how many emotions were hitting her all at once. Her dad had been there, watching out for her, protecting her. But a question had been plaguing her for an entire year. She couldn't just let it go.

"If you wanted to protect me so much, why did you get me into the mess in the first place? If you hadn't sent me those letters last year, I never would have found the box. I never would have figured out you went to Wellsworth. I never would have asked so many questions that made Jonas realize who I was."

Her dad tucked her hair behind her ear. "He already knew."

Emmy's heart skipped a pounding beat. "What do you mean? I thought he didn't know until I asked him about you."

"Well, that might be true, but he knew I had a twelve-year-old American daughter. He found out I was alive and had a family, but he didn't know your names or where we were. I had to run to keep you safe. But when John told me your mother was sending you to Wellsworth, everything changed. You were bound to tell someone you had a father named Tom who'd disappeared ten years before." He ran his fingers through her hair. "And you've got my red hair... It was only a matter of time before he put two and two together."

"So why not just tell me to stay away from him? Why send me clues all year long instead of just telling me the Order was dangerous?"

Her dad gave her a sad smile. "If you'd gotten a letter from your long-lost father saying a secret society was after you, would you have believed it?"

Emmy wanted to say yes. If she was honest with herself, she probably would have thought it was a cruel prank.

"I think it might have been worse if you had believed it," her dad said. "You would have been terrified of your new school, of trusting anyone. If you'd been scared and friendless, that would have put you in even more danger. I hoped you'd find friends. I hoped you'd find your courage. Was I wrong?"

It seemed like a genuine question.

She thought about Lola; her fierce loyalty and passionate spirit. And Jack, with his quick smile and instant acceptance.

"You weren't wrong." Tears were streaming down Emmy's face now. "You shouldn't have come here tonight. You shouldn't have been following me in King's Lynn all year. It's way too risky."

His eyes crinkled. "You're worth it."

Emmy stared into his eyes. There was something about them that felt like a memory. It wasn't the way they looked—they were the wrong color. Contacts probably. The memory was the way they looked *at her*. With all the love he could give her.

The car swerved again, and this time two other cars swerved behind them. Barlowe cleared his throat. "I'm so sorry to interrupt, but—"

"I see them." Her dad's smile had disappeared. "Take a hard right." The other two cars followed, and then another.

"They've got us," he muttered.

Emmy's arms started to shake. "Can't we get away?"

"They've got at least three cars on us already, and I bet every one of them is sending a GPS signal to their reinforcements. I'm sure they were well prepared tonight."

Emmy clutched onto her dad. She couldn't lose him. Not now. Not again.

Barlowe gunned the engine and weaved in and out of cars. "What's the plan?"

Her dad swallowed. "Blackfriars Bridge."

Barlowe glanced in the rearview mirror, then nodded.

Her dad rummaged through his satchel, pushing aside boxes until he found the one he wanted. He pulled out a canister and strapped it to his arm.

"What's that?"

"An air tank." He plugged a tube into the canister, attached another piece of plastic, and hid everything under his sleeve. "It will let me breathe underwater."

"Underwater?" Emmy didn't understand.

He put his hand on her cheek. "I won't be able to contact you for some time. But know that I love you," he whispered. "Don't ever question that."

Emmy felt the car clunk as it drove onto the bridge.

"I have to go," her dad whispered.

"Go where?" Emmy wanted to stop him. She wanted to ask just one of the millions of questions she'd never gotten to ask. She wanted just one more minute.

Her dad threw his satchel over his shoulder and put his hand on the door handle. "Let's do it."

Barlowe threw the steering wheel to the left and slammed

into the sidewalk. The door flew open and her dad leapt onto the railing. Emmy screamed. He didn't look back. He just disappeared over the edge.

Chapter 21

After the Fall

E mmy was still screaming when the car screeched back into traffic. "Stop! We have to go back!"

"The Order saw him fall," Barlowe said. "They're all about to descend on that spot."

Sure enough, three cars were already pulled up onto the sidewalk. Men were pointing their phones at the water, probably trying to see if her dad came back to the surface. Pedestrians were looking, too.

"Someone will have called the police, and we need to keep you away from that."

"Why?" Emmy sobbed.

"Do you want to explain why you were in a car with your father when he's been missing for ten years? Do you want to explain why he just threw himself off a bridge?"

Emmy shook her head. Explaining it to the police would be bad enough, but they'd call her mom. Explaining it to her would be a nightmare.

"I don't think any of those cars is following us." Barlowe kept looking in his rearview mirror. "Tom's the one they want."

"Is he going to be okay?"

"That air canister will let him travel miles downstream without coming to the surface. He'll be just fine."

Emmy wiped the tears off her face and shoved her hands under her knees. She wished she could be as confident as Barlowe.

"What about you?" Barlowe glanced at her. "Are you going to be okay?"

Emmy had no idea how to answer that. She was shaking so badly that her teeth were chattering.

"I think I'd better take you home," Barlowe said. "Where are you staying?"

Emmy pulled up Lucy's address on her phone, then sent Lola a text.

You guys okay?

Yeah. On our way to Jack's. Did your dad get away?

Emmy didn't answer. What if the Order was monitoring her phone somehow? She couldn't put in writing that her dad got away.

I can't talk about it right now.

Okay. I hope everything's all right. Call us when you get to Lucy's.

Okay.

Emmy brushed more tears off her face. She couldn't look a mess when she got to Lucy's house. She didn't want any questions.

Barlowe pulled the car in front of Lucy's town house and looked at her. "Your dad can take care of himself. I promise."

"Do you think he'll try to pretend he's dead again?" *If he's not actually dead.*

"I'm not sure," Barlowe said. "They're bound to be suspicious."

Emmy looked at her shaking hands. If they thought he was still alive, then none of this would be over.

"Emmy, there's nothing you can do for him now. You don't need to worry. I'll let you know as soon as I've heard from him."

"Does the Order know you're involved with my dad?"

Barlowe tapped his fingers on the steering wheel. "I'm not sure about that, either. They could have recognized me tonight. But if they had known before now, I'm sure they would have put some, shall we say, pressure on me to give him up. Let's hope they weren't looking at the driver's seat too closely." He gave her a tight smile.

Emmy tucked her hair behind her ear. Now Barlowe might be in danger, too.

"Do you want me to come in with you?" he asked.

"You're not even supposed to be in London," Emmy said. "If Lucy tells someone you were with me, the Order will be onto you."

His smile relaxed. "Thank you."

She got out of the car, went up the town house steps and opened the door. "Hello?" she called gingerly. She was not looking forward to a grilling from Lucy.

Lucy padded out of the kitchen. "You're alone."

Emmy blinked. "Um, yeah."

"Thank God," Lucy said. "I wasn't looking forward to my home being overrun with hooligans. Did they find somewhere else to stay, then? Please tell me they're not on their way."

"No," Emmy said, "they're staying somewhere else."

"Well, maybe next time you can stay with them, too."

Emmy just about groaned. The last thing she needed was to be in the same house as Donovan Galt. She opened her mouth to say something, then stopped.

Donovan Galt. Jack's father.

It didn't sound like he'd been one of the people following them, but he must have heard about what happened by now.

Emmy's heart beat faster. Barlowe was wrong. There was something she could do for her dad. If it worked, it might just save his life. And maybe get the Order off her back for good.

"Actually, I'm staying with them this time, too."

Lucy narrowed her eyes. "What?"

"I just came by to tell you that I'm staying at a friend's house, so you don't need to worry about me."

"You can't go traipsing around London like some kind of delinquent, and I'm certainly not driving you anywhere." Lucy whirled around and stomped up the stairs.

"Did I mention my friend's parents are members of the Thackery Club?"

Lucy froze. "You're lying."

"Their names are Donovan and Nadiya Galt." Emmy pulled up Jack's contact info on her phone and passed it to Lucy. "That's their address."

Lucy stared at the phone. "That's in Belgravia. It's one of the most exclusive streets in London."

"So... Can I go?"

Lucy hesitated. "Like I said, I'm not driving you anywhere, but I'll pay for your cab."

Emmy's knees wobbled as she stepped along the walkway that led to Jack's front door. She rang the bell and closed her eyes. Hopefully Jack and Lola wouldn't be too mad at her for what she was about to do. She'd texted them to say she was coming, but she couldn't tell them what was really going on, not yet. She needed their reactions to be real.

The heavy, black door opened wide. Jack and Lola were staring at her from the other side.

"What happened?" Jack whispered.

Images flashed in her mind. The men surrounding them in the gallery. The cars closing in on them. Her father diving off the bridge. Her dad.

Sobs started pouring out of her. She couldn't stop them if she tried. The story she was about to tell might not be totally true, but her feelings were. "He's dead."

Lola started crying and Jack pulled her into a tight hug.

"I'm so, so sorry," Jack said.

Emmy couldn't stop holding him.

Lola put her arms around both of them and buried her face in Emmy's shoulder. "We're both here."

Emmy didn't know if she'd ever heard Lola be so gentle. It made Emmy cry even harder.

"Why don't you bring her into the sitting room," said a voice from across the hall.

They all looked up. Jack's dad was standing in a doorway. His face didn't look hard like it usually did. His forehead was crinkled, and his eyes were soft. Almost like he was concerned about her.

Emmy didn't know what to think. Whatever Mr. Galt was feeling right now, it didn't change what she'd been through that night, and it didn't change the fact that it was the Order that had put her through it.

Jack and Lola held her hands as they went through an arched doorway on the right. Emmy pushed the door closed before Mr. Galt could follow them, then sank onto a couch and wiped her face with her sleeve.

"What happened?" Jack asked again.

"We tried to get away, but there were too many cars

following us." Emmy took a shuddering breath. "He…he said this would never be over for me as long as he was alive. That he couldn't keep putting me through this. He told the guy driving the car to pull over and"—Emmy brought the image of what happened next to her mind—"he jumped off the bridge."

Lola clamped her hand over her mouth and Jack started crying, too.

"Maybe he was just trying to get away," Jack said. "He might have swam to the shore."

Emmy glanced at the door. Even though she'd closed it tightly, now it was open a crack.

She shook her head. "He said if he died, his secrets died with him. And he had a heavy bag strapped around his shoulder. The current probably…probably…" Every fear Emmy had about what might have happened overwhelmed her and she started sobbing again.

"I'm going to get her some water," Jack said in a strangled voice.

Lola didn't say anything when Jack left. She just wrapped her arms around Emmy and cried with her.

A few minutes later they heard raised voices, then full-on shouting. They followed the sound up a short flight of steps and into a kitchen that seemed to be made entirely of black and white marble.

"How can you say that?" Jack was yelling at his father. "How can you say the Order isn't all bad when you saw what happened tonight? Emmy's dad is dead!"

"That's not what I would have wanted," Mr. Galt said. His tone was clipped and tight. "If he had just come quietly and given us the information we needed—"

Jack swore. It was the first time Emmy had heard him do that.

"John!" his dad said sharply.

"My name is Jack," he said through gritted teeth.

Mr. Galt's face went rigid. "As I was saying, there was no need for anyone to get hurt. Violence is not part of our nature."

"Then why did Jonas try to kill me last year?" Emmy said quietly.

Jack and Mr. Galt turned around. They hadn't even noticed Emmy and Lola come in.

Mr. Galt cleared his throat. "Young lady, that is absurd. I understand that you may have been frightened, but—"

"He came at me with a knife, and when I climbed down a rope to escape, he started to cut through it so I would fall onto the stone floor."

Mr. Galt blinked. He actually looked surprised.

"Then there's Lola," Emmy went on. "Did you know he paid people to beat her up?"

Mr. Galt shook his head. "I know Jonas can be headstrong sometimes, but he wouldn't harm children. I'm one of his closest advisors. I know him."

"So, you'll believe him before you'll believe your own son?" Jack asked.

Mr. Galt hesitated.

"If you're one of his closest advisors, then you must have known what was really going on tonight," Jack said.

"That's not how the Order works," Mr. Galt said. "Individual members rarely know the full scope of an assignment. That way, if anything goes wrong, we can deny knowing what was happening."

"Just like the mafia, right?" Jack said.

Mr. Galt narrowed his eyes at his son. "That's enough. Our family has been part of the Order of Black Hollow Lane for generations. We owe much of our fortune to them."

"I don't want your fortune," Jack said. "Not if we owe it to a bunch of street thugs."

"I am no thug." Mr. Galt was standing as straight as a pencil, his hands curled into fists. "Not everyone in the Order is as horrible as you seem to think. I find and preserve art work. It's a noble calling. Your skill as an artist could be useful to us."

"I'm not going to lift a single paintbrush to help them." He pointed at Emmy. "They as good as killed her father. Jonas tried to kill her. How can you look at her and still defend them?"

Emmy figured Mr. Galt would just walk away, but he didn't. He looked at her. Really looked at her. The lines on his face seemed to get deeper.

"If you'll excuse me," Mr. Galt said, "I need to make a phone call." He marched past them, head held high, as though his own son hadn't just called him a thug.

"Sorry about that," Jack mumbled.

"You were great," Lola said. "I'm glad you finally told him off."

"Yeah, well…" Jack looked down, his fingers twisting behind his back. That conversation couldn't have been easy for him.

"Has anybody looked at the footage from tonight?" Lola asked.

Emmy blinked. She'd completely forgotten she'd been wearing a camera all evening.

"I checked mine while you were getting changed," Jack said

dully. "There's nothing useful from the party. You can't even see the guys moving toward Emmy or anything."

"Um, did my camera record the stuff with my dad in the car?" Emmy asked.

Jack nodded. "I didn't look at that part, though."

That footage would show her dad strapping on an air canister and telling her he'd be fine. It would show Barlowe in the car. If the Order got ahold of it, it would be a disaster.

Footsteps sounded on the stairs, but it wasn't Mr. Galt.

"Oliver!" Jack stared at his brother, who seemed just as surprised to see him.

"What are you guys doing here?" Oliver said.

Jack, Emmy, and Lola glanced at each other.

"We, uh, we were at a party with Dad," Jack said.

Oliver tipped his head and frowned. "You were at Dad's event tonight? But I thought it was… I mean… You're not part of… Never mind."

Jack took a careful step toward him, and Oli shuffled his feet. He seemed to want to look anywhere but at Jack.

"Oli, do you know something about tonight?"

Oliver shook his head, looking at the floor.

"What did you mean when you said I'm not part of something?"

"Nothing," Oliver said quickly. "I was confused."

Jack took another step closer. "Oli, are you talking about the Order?"

Oliver's eyes flickered to Jack finally. He didn't ask what the Order was. He didn't say no. There was nothing about Jack's question that was surprising to him.

"I didn't know Dad had told you about it already," Jack said softly. "That's why he wants you in Latin Society, right?"

Oliver nodded. He still couldn't meet Jack's gaze.

"They're really dangerous, Oli. They'll turn you into a different person. Make you do things you don't want to."

Oliver glanced at Lola, and then back at the ground.

"You need to be your own person." Jack put his hand on his brother's shoulder. "No matter what anybody says, you don't have to join."

Finally, Oliver raised his eyes to Jack's and looked at him for a long moment. "Yeah. I do."

There were more footsteps on the stairs. Mr. Galt was finally back. "I have been asked to inform you that Miss Boyd is about to be readmitted to Wellsworth."

All four of them gasped and Lola grabbed Jack's arm.

"Are you serious?" she asked.

"How?" Jack's eyes were narrow and hard.

"The real culprit is going to confess to it being a prank, and that he didn't think Miss Boyd would get in so much trouble." He looked at Oliver. "Which is essentially the truth, isn't it?"

Everyone turned toward Oliver, who was staring at his slippers.

"Oli?" Jack whispered.

Oliver didn't say anything.

"You're the thief? You took the White Stone Gate money?"

Tears slipped down Oliver's face.

"Don't be too hard on him," Mr. Galt said. "He's got a difficult confession ahead of him."

Lola's eyes went wide. "You're going to let your own son get expelled for something you told him to do?"

"Expelled?" Mr. Galt shook his head. "Of course not. The board would never allow that to happen."

"How could you do this to him?" Jack said. "How could you ask him to do something like that?"

"He's not the one who asked me," Oliver mumbled. "I didn't even think he knew."

"I didn't know," Mr. Galt said softly. "We tend not to know too much about what other members are doing. Brother Loyola prefers it that way. Someone explained the full situation to me just now on the phone."

Emmy pressed her lips together. Mr. Galt was the one who got his eleven-year-old kid involved in a secret society. He definitely wasn't innocent in all this.

Mr. Galt put his hands on Oliver's shoulders and crouched down to look him in the eye. "This will all be taken care of," he whispered. "The Order always takes care of its own."

Oliver didn't say anything. He just kept staring at the floor.

Mr. Galt stood up. "As I was saying, Miss Boyd should be readmitted tomorrow and can return to classes on Monday."

"What's the catch?" Emmy didn't bother to keep the skepticism out of her voice.

Mr. Galt swallowed. "There's no catch, Miss Willick. Our people at the bridge saw your father struggling in the water tonight. The currents dragged him under. I'm sorry to tell you that he really is gone."

Emmy stared at the floor. Her dad must have put on a good show. As soon as he went under, he would have stuffed the breathing tube into his mouth and let the current pull him downstream until it was safe to swim to shore.

"Because your father is dead, there's no possibility of retrieving the information that was apparently being asked of you. Since you cannot get what Jonas wants, we have decided to pursue other avenues. You are no longer of any interest to the Order."

Emmy's knees buckled and she grabbed onto the kitchen counter. She did it. She was finally free of them, and hopefully her dad was, too.

"Why did Jonas get me back into Wellsworth?" Lola asked. "It couldn't be out of the goodness of his heart."

"It wasn't," Mr. Galt said shortly. "It was at the insistence of one of his closest advisors." He turned and went back down the stairs with Oliver following close behind.

"Come on," Jack said to Emmy, "let's get you up to bed. Do you want your own room, or do you want to bunk with Lola?"

"With Lola." The last thing Emmy wanted was to be alone.

Jack led them up four flights of stairs to the very top of the house.

"Can you come and hang out for a few minutes?" Emmy asked Jack.

"Sure."

Emmy closed the door behind him and locked it. She ripped off her cardigan and yanked the camera out of the buttonhole.

"Em, what are you—"

"Get your cameras," she whispered as she pulled off the

battery pack that was taped to her side. "Your dad doesn't know we have these, right?"

Jack shook his head. He pulled the camera out of his jacket while Lola found hers in the dress that was lying on the floor.

"Give me the SD cards." Emmy popped the cover off the battery pack and pulled out the SD card. She dropped it on the floor and crushed it with her heel.

"What the bloody hell is going on?" Lola hissed.

Emmy grabbed the SD card out of her hand and smashed that one, too. Then she grabbed Jack's and did the same.

"There's no chance the footage was sent anywhere else, right?"

"No," Jack said, "the cameras are totally self-contained."

Emmy took a long, deep breath. "So, you want to hear what really happened tonight?"

Chapter 22

Going Home

Lola was pretty mad when Emmy told them the truth. "Why didn't you just tell us? We could have played along."

"I needed your reactions to be totally real," Emmy said. "I knew Jack's dad would be listening at the door. I needed him to believe that my dad really is dead this time."

"I guess it worked," Jack said quietly. He was sitting on the bed, leaning his head against the wall.

"I'm sorry you had such a huge fight with your dad," Emmy said.

"I'm not," Jack said. "I never would have said those things if I hadn't been so angry, and if I hadn't said them, he might not have convinced Jonas to back off of you."

Jack was right. Emmy owed him a lot.

"So, what does it feel like, to be free of the Order?" Jack asked.

Emmy closed her eyes. "I don't know if it's hit me yet."

"Well, it's definitely hit me," Lola said. "I'm never setting foot at Erindale again."

They stayed up talking a while longer. Emmy fell asleep on top of the bed covers, listening to the sounds of her friends' voices.

It was nearly noon by the time they padded downstairs the next day.

"Looks like Mum's sent me about a million texts this morning," Lola said as she looked at her phone. "I guess she heard I'm back at Wellsworth."

"Sam sent a message asking if we're okay," Jack said. "So… Are we? Okay, I mean?"

The three of them looked at each other. They were going back to their school together. Going back home together.

"Yeah," Emmy said. "I think we are."

Jack grinned. "I'll let Sam know."

Emmy felt a familiar swoop in her stomach. She was still plenty mad at Sam, but she had a few other feelings for him, too.

They went up the little steps at the back of the house and into the kitchen. They all froze at the top of the stairs. Oliver was holding the fridge door open, looking anywhere but at the three of them.

The room was totally quiet. Nobody seemed to know what to say.

Finally, Lola broke the silence. "Morning, Oli. Did you have breakfast yet?"

Oliver's eyebrows shot up. "Um, no."

"Great," Lola said as she marched into the kitchen. "I make killer French toast. It's the one thing my dad can make that doesn't taste like shriveled-up tree bark." She started pulling ingredients out of the fridge, pretending not to notice everyone staring at her.

"Why...why are you doing that for me?" Oliver finally said.

Lola looked him square in the face. "We're your friends, and you need to know that the Order isn't your only option."

He looked at his hands, but Emmy could see the corners of his mouth turn up.

Oli helped make breakfast, but he only ate a few bites before he went upstairs. It would probably be awkward with him for a while.

Mr. Galt had left two boxes of pastries on the counter, and between those and the French toast, Emmy's stomach was soon stuffed to the brim with sugar.

Lola groaned and clutched her middle. "Why did I have that last Danish?"

"Because you can't resist sour cherries on anything," Emmy said. Her phone dinged and she pulled it out of her pocket. It was an email from Master Barlowe:

> Good afternoon, Miss Willick. I just thought I should let you know that the book I ordered for you has arrived safe and sound. You can pick it up on Monday.

Emmy breathed out. Barlowe hadn't ordered any book for her. He was telling her that her dad was safe. And hopefully, now that the Order really and truly thought he was dead, he always would be.

Emmy pulled her knees up to her chest. She'd tell Jack and Lola later. After all, she was still in Donovan Galt's house. She couldn't give up all her secrets quite yet. There would be plenty of time to talk when they got back to school. Plenty of time to sit in the common room and talk, or play games, or do all the things normal kids got to do. It would be nice to be normal for a change.

"What?" Lola yelled as she stared at her phone. "Mum says I'm not getting my spot back on the football team! I'm going to have to be a reservist!"

"Well, it wouldn't be fair to kick the new girl off," Jack said.

Lola tossed her phone on the table. "I'd rather stuff myself in a steak and kidney pudding than sit on the bench."

Emmy giggled. Well, maybe they'd never be *totally* normal. Whatever they were, they'd be okay. Because they were together.

Acknowledgments

None of this would be possible without the amazing team at Sourcebooks. To my editor, Annie Berger, thank you for giving so much careful thought to this project, and Sarah Kasman, thank you for your constant critical eye. To Cassie Gutman and Rebecca Sage, thank you for forgiving my incessant Canadian spellings and for spotting things I never would have seen. To Jordan Kost and Hannah Peck, thank you so much; your cover art is nothing less than astonishing. To the entire marketing team, especially Stefani Sloma, Heather Moore, and Lizzie Lewandowski, thank you for how you have championed this series. Special thanks to Fernanda Viveiros and everyone at Raincoast Books for working so hard in the Canadian market.

To my agent, Melissa Edwards, thank you for constantly pushing me to dig deeper into stories, and for the way you fight for those stories once they finally hit the page. To my beloved Pitch Wars MG crew, I can't imagine doing any of this without you. Special thanks to Kit Rosewater, Tara Creel, Lacee Little, Alli Jayce, Liz Edelbrock, and Gabby Byrne. Your endless support and endless critiques are constantly making me better, both as a writer and as a human.

To Joel, Tracy, and Benjamin, thank you for always giving me a home away from home. To Karl, Steph, and Matthew, thank you for the joy and light you always bring into my life. To Katherine, I'm sure you don't remember this, but when you read the first draft of what eventually became *The Mystery of Black Hollow Lane*, you sparked an idea that became central to the plot of this novel. I guess I owe you one.

To Judy, thank you for sparking my love of middle grade when we walked through Beacon Books that day. Auntie Lil, thank you for how you make all of us smile. Dad, thank you for the way you love each of us, and for how Audrey lights up every time she hears your name. Mom, I love you.

To my precious Audrey, thank you for being so generous with your love. You bring me joy every single day. And Jason, thank you for never, ever giving up.

About the Author

Julia Nobel is a teacher on an island off the south coast of Canada. By the time she was ten, she had a beloved notebook filled with plot ideas for novels and TV shows. Even though she hadn't read them in years, she cried when she had to get rid of her Baby-Sitters Club books because they wouldn't fit in the family's moving truck, and she promptly bought them all again in her new city. Now, she carries around another plot-filled notebook, although it's also filled with shopping lists and reminders to feed the cat. She is a writing coach and offers workshops for children, teens, and adults.